COMPANY TIME
v1.0

A geeky novel

by Jay Gross
author of *The Naked Ghost*

AmiGadget Press

Lexington, South Carolina

2011

COMPANY TIME v1.0
A geeky novel
by Jay Gross

ISBN 978-1-879211-03-2

For information regarding rights or licensing, contact the copyright holder at AmiGadget Press, PO Box 1696, Lexington, SC 29071, or visit blog.jaygross.com.

First printing: December 2011

Also by Jay Gross:
   The Naked Ghost, a novel. AmiGadget Press. May 2011.

Published by:
   AmiGadget Press
   P.O. Box 1696
   Lexington, SC 29071

   www.amigadget.com

for Amigans

Acknowledgements

Special thanks to the Twisted Scribes Writing Group, Fran Rizer, Ray Wade, John Koelsch and the late Leonard Jolley. Thanks also to Thierry Grenier, John Ramspot, Dana Dominiak, Joy Smith, Ivan Taylor, Aimeric Barthe and Jay Reed. They spurred me along in the creative process one way or another, whether they knew it or not.

Chapter 1 : Bots for bots' sake

*T*he systems analyst never mingles, never visits. He sends curt email, usually implying that your request for an audience with him squanders that most valuable of company resources, his time. Therefore, request denied. Problem? Your replacement is filling out the application for employment right now. The systems analyst rarely meets your gaze, neither in your space nor even in his. Some say the systems analyst's aloofness is on account of his exalted, nay, exulted position. Some say it's his OCD asserting itself in the stressful work environment. Indeed, some call his hands-off, memos-on style of management a blessing from merciful deities. Some say he's just a geek abusing hard-won power. Others snarl that his spouse keeps him tethered to the water pipes at night and he compensates by bullying people at the office. Company know-it-alls even claim the elusive systems analyst is really a robotic computer program–a "bot" in the trade. Its non-human, ether-bound electronic presence demands and collects senseless emailed project reports, then automatically re-emails them to interminable lists of nameless higher-ups tucked away in some yet more distant cubicles, operated in turn by other bots.

Within the Kramden Software Company, a teetering chess-like assembly of power pieces take their turns at play–no, at *foreplay*. Plotting, planning, organizing their attack at that elusive archenemy, competition–leading, they hope, to a spurting orgasm of profit and ever more power–though perhaps instead to debilitating ignominy replete with recriminations, layoffs, indictments and loss. The power pieces rule, namely the product managers, section supervisors and systems analysts. The lowly, thankful pawns, namely the geeky program coders, serve.

Wishfully upward-mobile, the coders kowtow to those electronic bots and memos, eager to impress their superiors by tap-tapping computer languages in endless legions of industrial-carpeted, intraneted cubicles. Namely, geek cocoons. Drab and mostly windowless, these pods of the software development hive are spun of polyester fibers game for the touch of Velcro-laden artifacts. Like the ceilings, the furnishings and the floors, they're sound absorbent. If a virtual tree falls in a virtual forest of such cubicles, only a few cubes away there would be no sound at all, no flutter, not even a whisper. That is, unless someone notified Security or tipped off the company gravevine.

In their gray sea, this motley bunch of lowly pawns, the program coders dignified as software engineers, make the megalithic Kramden Company's vaporous software applications actually work—in spite of the interference of management, in spite of the hyper-developed company political system and the company grapevine, in spite of the org charts and the re-org charts, the network crashes and the manifold layers of security safeguards. In spite of the bots, or perhaps to spite them. And in spite of the systems analysts.

{ }

Fourteen rows, twelve, ten... nine rows of cubicles... It's one of those exceptions to the rule that the systems analyst never visits the gray maze. A dress-down Friday, it's a special day—like rif days, only not as scary. Rif means "Reduction In Force." Those occur when Nineteenth Floor—meaning management in their distant HQ edifice—has made enough blunders to get the stockholders mad, or when the Board of Directors, nigh onto deities, ordains from on high (floor forty in another, yet more distant glass tower) that productivity shall increase such that the stock price shall flutter upward, making them even richer.

This casual dress day, however, even in the absence of curt rif layoff notices accompanied by a run on the office laserprinters to churn out job hunting materials—today, the Almighty Systems Analyst Himself, Mister Ozzie G. Osgood, for whom the G might as well stand for "God," marches smartly, starched crisp and steam ironed, through the rows of cubicles, like a jungle cat ready to pounce. A trail of awe precedes him, and a collective sigh of relief follows him through the aisles. Five rows... Four... A path of conjecture and gossip eddies just out of earshot in his wake. The smell of power oozes from his well scrubbed pores. The fragrance of designer cologne pervades his space and eddies around him.

"Morning, sir."

Nod. Sneer.

"Morning."

Nod. Smirk.

"G'morning."

Silence. The systems analyst digests lowly programmers for lunch, picks their blithering remains from his teeth, and moves on to the next repast. You do not request or even encourage an actual presence of the systems analyst if you are in your right mind, and if you are in your right mind when and if he shows up at your cubicle you probably won't be for long. Stock up on Tums or hundred-proof courage as you choose. Besides, people in their right minds don't work for Kramden Software Company. People in their right minds work somewhere else, for someone else, for some other systems analyst at some other company. Until rif day.

{ }

Trailed by murmurs and surrounded by a cloud of nervous tap-tapping on keyboards, he appeared. The almighty systems analyst, Osgood himpersonalself showed up in actual person at John Farmer's gray-flannel cubicle, a quizzical look on his face and a permanent case of serious attitude etched into his stance. Obviously, he brought his ego along, in its entirety.

"You rang?" Osgood accused. "I've got a ten o'clock and a ten-thirty, so let's make this snappy. I don't see why I couldn't just call up your program on the network and handle this in email as always."

{ }

No dress-down days for Osgood, ever, and this was no exception. Perfectly tailored, meticulously groomed. Crisp white shirt. Perfectly knotted, pin-striped, Italian silk tie. Perfectly fitted jacket. All gray. Black Italian shoes with a polish the envy of any self-assured mirror. The other amazing thing was that he didn't launch into his standard productivity rap: *Meetings take time. Time is money. Meetings are a waste of money–company money–if you spend company time in useless meetings. Meetings mean k-lines don't increment. K-lines keep the department operating. Don't ask about it, don't question it, just code it. Next item.*

{ }

In Geekspeak, a "k-line" is a thousand and twenty-four lines of programming code, arcane programming verbiage replete with punctuation sprinkled liberally, like pepper on a blackened fish. A thousand and twenty-four lines of gibberish– namely, some computer language that when compiled, tweaked, debugged, revised, rewritten, discarded and redone from start makes something happen on some screen, over some network, across some cloud-bound connection, with someone's permission, after someone presses any key, under Security's watchful gaze. It's a thousand and twenty-four, not a simple thousand, because powers of two, which a thousand-and-twenty-four is one of, rule computers. And coders.

Large computer programs require many thousands, even millions, of lines of code. Computer hardware by itself does nothing, and it does a lot of it, though it looks pretty doing it. Software makes it work, makes it do even the most rudimentary things. If you want something to move across the screen, you have to create software that does it. Then you have to create more software that takes in information from the user and translates it to commands that make the object move. You want something calculated? Computers are only as adept at math as the programs make them. To keep track of information, you need information programs like spreadsheets and database managers. To balance your checkbook, you need software than adds–or subtracts, as the case may be.

Large programs relegate repeating tasks to small "routines," and an oversight program arranges stacks of them to do the users' bidding. Every action, no matter how small, requires some computer code to do it. Even if it's built into the operating system, a program has to "call" the OS and invoke the feature. So, few k-lines means not much code, and not much progress toward the lofty goal of shipping the software to the testers and-slash-or the end users–meaning the customers. A thousand lines of faulty code is a problem, not a benefit. Indeed, a handful of lines of brilliant code often do a better job than many k-lines of uninspired geeksmanship. Nonetheless, the cubicle crowd deifies k-lines because HR bestows intense importance on them as a measure of productivity. HR is Human Resources, the source and signee for paychecks. And rif notices. HR doesn't speak compulingo, just bean counting. And k-lines.

{ }

Ego and attitude abundant, there stood Osgood, tall and fit, his posture as perfect as his blond, fashionably cut hair. Yet, impatience and all, his nervous twitch was also present. Always was. Just enough of an eye twitch underneath all that arrogance, composure and cologne, underneath all that designer clothing, all that cocksuredness, to communicate even to the mere earthlings he ruled that Systems Analyst Osgood was, someday, going to crack.

"Thanks for coming over. This won't take long," John said loud, confident. Loud was John's usual. When John spoke people listened, even if they didn't want to. Half a head shorter than Osgood, fit like the avid rock climber he was and geekly handsome, John didn't speak unless he had something to say. Then he said it. Loud. Always loud. Had something to do with earphones and rock and roll. People whispered that it had to do with recreational drugs, too. Not true. Computers were John's drugs. Computers and music. Loud. Besides, recreational drug use went against Sections 25-6a and 26-1c of the *Kramden Company Policy Manual*, subject to random tests, the successful passing of which was required to maintain even the lowest security clearance. "Here, have a seat." John offered his own comfy gray chair in front of the large workstation in his cubicle.

In the cubicles around John's, silence presided like stones in a cemetery. Nervous clicks of keyboards and mousebuttons muffled off the stoic half-walls as lowly programmers pretended to be hard at work racking up those k-lines, parked their solitaire, Age of Dungeon Quests games and other things more entertaining than program code or this week's emergency rewrites. Guilt-ridden and annoyed, they stashed their incriminating windows behind officious looking screens of complex computer code, sat quiet, and strained to overhear. Eavesdropping, a revered tradition at Kramden Company, paid off in ways other than k-lines, though sometimes in rifs.

"This better be good, and it better be worth my time," Osgood warned, hovering over the empty chair, not seating himself. He cast a glance over the cubicle wall into the next space.

Appearing hard at work, on purpose, Jerry Branson faked a frown at his screen, fingered the voluminous *Kramden Company Manual for Source Code Commentary*, making sure the tome's title would be visible from over the cubicle wall in case his boss peeked in, and tap-tapped random punctuation into the ether, feigning deep thought every few keystrokes. A buxom blonde wearing a wicked smile and nothing else lurked, safely obscured by rows of k-lines in the making, awaiting a forward over the company intranets to several like-minded colleagues under the subject "Tuesday's meeting notes." Branson collected the good images over a day's time, executed a surreptitious save to optical–that is, a CD or DVD rom disc–to join dozens of other optical and flex disks–floppies– in his personal effects drawer until he could manage to extricate them from the building. Veronica–pictured in the snapshot on his desk–would hardly approve of his "collection," but what she doesn't know won't hurt him.

{ }

Kramden employee policy permits one drawer of personal effects, and one drawer only. For security reasons, anything not stored in your personal effects drawer is considered company property. Period. Privacy of your personal effects drawer is neither promised nor afforded, all areas of all cubicles being subject to security inspection at any time for any reason. Or no reason at all. Optical and flex disks are always company property, no matter their origin, even if you store them in your personal effects drawer, a practice that is highly discouraged, but not subject to disciplinary action. All flex disks, no matter where they are, must be formatted on Kramden computers to Kramden standards, meaning they will thenceforth read and write only on Kramden computers–company policy manual Section 7-1a, *et seq*. Possession of any media formatted to work on non-

Kramden computers is a firing offense–Section 7-9a. If you succeed in taking a flex disk out of the building, it wouldn't work in any other computer, and they're not permitted out of the building anyway, so don't even try it. Security stations will immediately format flex disks to Kramden requirements on entry to the building, so don't even try that, either. Opticals are subject to inspection, too, and must not contain any company data, or anything that looks like it. Because of the extremely sensitive nature of Kramden's defense contracts, programmers may not take company files home, either by physical media such as flex and optical disks or by memory devices or by email to outside addresses.

According to Branson, none of this applies to him, since his job description makes him a fairly important part of the security system itself. He implements security measures on the company networks to prevent *other people* from removing files from the building. Branson's enviable and secret access to the outside world is enabled by his high-level clearances as administrator and architect of the intra-company networks that connect the departments together in a virtual maze. He looks out for his personal needs when he edits the software that monitors the intranets. He's careful with flex disks, storing in his personal drawer only the ones that contain only personal information, most of it gleaned from the *alt.sex.binaries...* hierarchy and elsewhere on the public nets. Few people in the company know the extent of his powers, but several partake of his generosity in sharing his gleanings.

The security station at the building's employee entrance is empowered and required to unleash their bots to examine the contents of any computer files that you wish to take out of the building and to retain a printout of the filenames in a sealed, dated envelope, establishing a provable date on which the information existed and was removed from the building–useful in the event of a dispute (translate: litigation) over their ownership or existence. Assuming the bots report that the source medium contains no Kramden intellectual property, source code or programs, Security is required to copy the files, using a duplicator, not a computer, onto a memory device that you provide. They then store the original in a sealed, dated envelope. This policy retains company control of all computer files and all Kramden-formatted flex disks. Warning: any attempt to subvert the system results in instant dismissal (Section 7-26f(c.1–5)) on security grounds, the most heinous sin that can be committed at Kramden.

Branson isn't worried about the rigors of getting files out of the building. He games the system by ingeniously storing his files compressed and encrypted, encapsulating them in seemingly innocuous matter like stock reports, Team Kramden volleyball rosters and tax forms. The results always sail right through Security's scrutiny, a boon to Branson's collection of "artistic" materials as well as to his continued employment.

After the famous international incident over Iranian computers being corrupted by virii brought in on USB memory devices, the company no longer permits such devices in the building, much less plugged into company computers. You may leave them with the Security desk.

{ }

"If you'll be so kind as to log in to the system and do a few basic commands?" Loud. "So that my program can identify your style." John flipped his longish, reddish hair away from his intense, green eyes with a snap of the neck. He pulled his gray plastic side chair over to the workspace. His boss's quick frown bade him leave it unoccupied. John sat down anyway.

Osgood bent over the terminal and pointedly looked over his shoulder as he logged into the section's server. John pointedly looked away while Osgood tapped passwords.

"Okay, I'm in," Osgood condescended. "You want simple stuff like "ls" and "pwd" or something more complicated? As you know I can get as complicated as you like." He typed a few complex commands confidently, never having to backspace, and smacking the Return key with a vengeance. "Is this going to take us anywhere? And soon? We're using company time, here."

"I didn't want to intrude on personal time, yours or mine, though I think the company might be interested in this. It's a whole new software technology that I've just begun to explore. A whole new paradigm, which as you know is exactly twenty cents. One or three more, please." Loud. Smile.

Osgood ignored the pun and typed fast and precise. "One or three," he repeated. "So you're recording this with a background program? Sniff my passwords by having me type them at your terminal? Old trick," he accused. "This is one of my demo accounts. I'd never enter my root-access passwords from someone else's terminal. It would be dumber than dumb and a major breach of security."

"Of course not," said John, loud, still smiling patiently. "You know me better than that, Oz."

Osgood frowned, looked around.

John stood up and pressed on in his normal, loud tone. "My program has nothing to do with passwords, but if you'll just chill for another two or five seconds you'll see something that I guarantee to amaze and astound."

Osgood tapped his watch. "So said your email. So amaze and astound me, and now. I've got things to do."

"You can stop typing."

Osgood had already removed his hands from the keyboard.

John leaned over the desk and clicked a mousebutton. His workstation's ginormous monitor accommodated many programs, each running in a little window and color coded according to a complex hierarchy that John imposed. A garish graphic clock beamed from the screen's top left corner. Its animated red second hand marked time with precise jumps between lime green Kramden Company logos that marked the hours. Other windows displayed rows of numbers and letters, snippets of arcane computer source code with blocks highlighted in yellow, others in blue. "Now, if I were to ask you to type something else," John said, loud, slow, "what command would you type?"

"Well, I'm losing patience fast, but I suppose if I typed anything else, and I'm frankly not very inclined to do much else, I'd maybe do... a simple 'ls minus la' to maybe list the slash-bin directory yet again, pipe it to 'more' for good measure and that's about it, really. This is getting to be quite enough. No, it's too much." Osgood put his hands out to type again, but John waved him back and touched the mousebutton, poised and confident. A small window titled "Predictive Analysis v0.9.0.1e" appeared near the pointer. Its maroon background bore clean white text. "This is the command you would have entered?"

"Mmmm probably. So?"

John clicked the mouse, making other commands appear in the window. "So, if you were to keep entering commands, these ones scrolling in this red window are exactly what you'd enter next, are they not?" He smiled, benign and confident, clicking again and again. Lines of text appeared—some simple, only two characters, and some containing many characters and punctuation marks— the picky command language of computers at their lowest level.

"Could be." Osgood scanned the window. "So is this a mind reader program for the command shell? Great marketing potential there, John." Osgood's eye twitched. "We'll make a pair of dimes or a quarter on it, easy. Amortized over a century or more, that is. I can sooo picture DoD lining up for custom versions."

{ }

Pronounced *DEE-OH-DEE* and mostly spoken with requisite awe, "DoD" is Kramden Software lingo for "Tooth Fairy," namely the United States Department of Defense. The admirals and generals funnel vast amounts of green to Kramden for exotic software with customized extras: extra security, extra secrecy, extra performance, extra features, extra-extra security, extra all of the above and extra everything else, and extra don't ever tell anyone about any of this. Ever. DoD is the main reason for all the security concerns, the security testing, the security tracking, and the security blitzes that keep HR busy hiring new programmers. The DoD takes a system-wide approach. No single person is permitted to know the entire scope and methods of a project. No single group is permitted to develop more than a third of any project's software, and all projects have multiple identities, multiple sets of requirements, and frequently "ghost" developments that are never intended to be part of the final project, never even intended to work, just thrown in to throw off anyone trying to fathom any of it. The Kramden Company Security Manual describes security policies in some detail, but even the manual itself is considered a security risk, so it lives in restricted places on the company network servers, and no part of it is permitted to be committed to paper, ever.

{ }

John smiled, patient. "Well, at some point fairly soon you'd try to fool my program, and you'd start adding weird switches, funny parameters that you'd hope I might not even know. Wouldn't you?" John pointed to one of the more unusual punctuation-laden commands at the end of the scrolling list.

"Undoubtedly," Osgood grumped, watching the commands with increasing nervousness and a strong eye twitch.

"Then about..." click-click-click "now... yes, there's a really esoteric one. How am I doing so far?"

"I don't know what you're trying to do, so how can I say how you're doing? Look, why don't you just skip the drama and tell me the meaning of this, and now? Before you waste any more of your time and mine–Kramden Company time in both cases, I remind you. And besides that, detail for me exactly how any of this is going to benefit your assigned projects? And meet your production schedule? Which is, if I remember right, today?" The last question was definitely a threat.

"Okay, it's like this. My program is able to predict what someone is going to type far into the future. It can even predict exactly when the stuff they enter will become unpredictable, and for you, I'm surprised to say, that's a matter of not just minutes, but days."

"Predict the unpredictability of predictable predictions?" Osgood looked like he was preparing to laugh, but he glued his gaze to the screen, his eye twitching with each line that John clicked into the window. "How are you–?"

John clicked the mousebutton. Fast. "I'm using system commands to demonstrate, but the program predicts any input. Anything and everything. For example, it can predict the content of your letters, entries you make in your project journals, your progress reports, even program source code hundreds or even thousands of lines into the future. Do you see now? These are exactly correct, aren't they? I can tell they're correct by how they're making you extremely nervous."

Osgood sat down. His eye twitch shook his whole face. "Correct? Yes, they're correct, down to the last tilde, but so what? And yes, they do make me nervous. Extremely, as you say." He stood up. "And like I said, so what?" Twitch. He sat down again. "We're still wasting resources, here." Osgood tapped his watch. "Company resources?"

On pretense of consulting a dusty volume of network protocols from a corner shelf, Branson edged his chair closer to John's cubicle wall.

John scrolled the window quickly. "See... looks like we're far enough into the future now to predict what you'll type at your office terminal after lunch." He clicked the mousebutton. "There's your root-level login name... see?" Click. "And your password. That is your correct password? All twenty-four characters? Root access?"

{ chapter 1 }

Chapter 2 : Security!

Osgood stood up halfway and flopped back down, fidgeting in the chair. He watched the screen at John's workstation, his face crimson, his gaze intent, his eye twitch violent.

With a grin, John hurried on. "Since we're still here in the present, and since what I'm showing you occurs in the future, your future self knows that your password is not secure, so..." John clicked the mousebutton "you're going to change it."

">KC_Passwd:" A command window appeared. Its deep blue cursor blinked, inviting, beside the Predictive Analysis screen.

John turned his back. "I won't watch. Triple-click and close the shell when you're done."

"Change password? Damn right." Osgood resized the window to a single line, hunched close to the keyboard to hide his keystrokes from no one around, and typed slow, heavy. "Okay, this charade has gone far enough. No, it's gone too far. Way too far. I'm looking at a serious security breach right here and now, and you've got some explaining to do, Mister Farmer. And I mean right now."

{ }

Kramden protocol is, in general, first names—see page 151 of the *Kramden Company New Employe* [sic] *Welcome Orientation and HR Policy Handbook,* revision 23.6.6.4a, hot off HR's megasized Xerox on the occasion of any newbies coming through the security gate. Not covered in the handbook, but company-wide practice, last names are reserved for ceremonial occasions like promotions, Team Kramden volleyball trophy presentations, firings and good-bye's on the inevitable rif days.

{ }

"You know I'm really supposed to immediately report this to Security?" The systems analyst checked his watch against the clock in the corner of the screen.

"Mister Osgood," said Mister Farmer, loud, "your password is quite secure, because you just changed it, but of course you should change it again from your office terminal, and I'm sure you will. Only you and I know what it was, and I was here in your presence the entire ten or thirty seconds it was compromised. Anyway–" John brought the maroon window to the front. "These predictive lines are currently only being displayed, not executed or stored, so there's no security breach at all. Your new password is just as secure as your old one."

Osgood's whole red face twitched rapidly. "Which, Mister Farmer, I see is apparently not very secure at all."

"Oz, you know and I know nothing is ever perfectly secure, notwithstanding what we tell the DoD. And you know I would never even consider using your system accounts for anything." John removed his glasses to polish them with the tail of his black and purple *The Safe Sax Sons* band T-shirt, tugging his clothes into even more disarray than usual.

Osgood rubbed his face. "John, if I didn't trust you implicitly, Security would be escorting you to the door now, and I mean *right now*, not ten microseconds in the future."

In the adjacent cubicle, Branson turned a page, which he wasn't reading.

"I'm sure." John replaced his glasses and clicked the mouse to bring up other system commands. "I'm really sorry I had to do that, but I needed something dramatic to convince you this is real. Bear with me just a little longer, please. I promise there is no danger to security." He expanded the prediction window. "See? My program knows you'll try to expunge this session from the history files, and it's already predicted those commands. You can execute all of it from here. Just copy from this red window and set up a background task in a shell. You haven't typed these yet, but you might as well make the predictions come true. Just hit Enter."

"And if I don't?"

John grinned, shrugged. "You can't *not* do it. I mean, you really can't help fulfilling what my program predicts, no matter what you try to do and no matter how hard you try. Odd as it sounds, so far I've found that it's always one hundred percent. Whatever it predicts *will* come true, no matter how seemingly farfetched. However, you don't have to physically go through the task of typing the stuff. You can just paste blocks as I've just suggested. It's like executing a macro in a word processor, or giving a simple shell command that has been aliased to something big and complicated. Saves work, and fulfills the predicted history. Or rather the predicted future, depending on your perspective. Go ahead and try not to do it. You'll see what I mean."

"Right." Osgood stuffed his hands in his pockets and glared over his shoulder at John.

"You can't change the future any more than you can change the past. If you somehow fail to do exactly what the program predicts, the program learns from its error and adjusts its further predictions accordingly. It actually works to the program's advantage if you try to fool it, because it can analyze your strategy. Just like in chess. The grand masters study their opponents' past games for mistakes and use that knowledge to plan their attack."

Thoughtful, quiet, Osgood captured the mouse and stood up, clutching it to his stomach. "You can shut this thing off?"

"Of course."

"Do it. Now. Erase all traces of this program from the entire system immediately, before the company backup process can commit it all to optical storage if it hasn't already. Mister Farmer, that is not a request. I trust you understand?"

"Certainly. But, fascinating isn't it? As well as scary? My program I mean, and what it can do?"

"I'm neither frightened nor fascinated nor convinced," Osgood said, "and I can't see how wasting your time and my time, Kramden Company time, has benefited the company or me or you. It certainly hasn't advanced your assigned tasks, and my week's progress report will reflect that fact." Osgood put down the mouse and examined his fingernails for dirt. *Twitch.* "I don't mind telling you, John, you're on very shaky territory." For emphasis, he tapped the keyboard–Return–executing the command tree. Osgood grimaced.

John glanced over the cubicle wall at Jerry Branson, who was typing furiously at his terminal. Most unusual. He turned to Osgood. "You've just macro'd the

list that my program predicted you would type. It was inevitable, like I said."
He executed another command tree. "There. That will expunge the program
and free its resources within a few seconds. Anyway, my present assignment
has definitely already benefited from this new Predictive Analysis, as you'll see
shortly. Besides, I see lots of potential applications for the technology, and I
definitely see DoD lining up, drooling to get hold of it–although you know how
I feel about my energies being diverted to warmaking."

Osgood shrugged, dallied with the mouse. "If this isn't a hoax–"

"So, disregarding any military applications for a moment, my predictive
system would be excellent for detecting attempts to fool Security long before
they occur. It could accurately predict the behavior of new employees, or perhaps
detect bugs in our programs way before anyone found them. A customer could
sit at a terminal, make all kinds of mistakes, and still run our products perfectly."

"We already have excellent spell checkers in the system software." Osgood
tugged his sleeve into just the right position to reveal exactly the correct amount
of shirt cuff.

"True, but we don't apply them to command line entries." John clicked the
mouse. "Not automatically, anyway."

"We could. Not a bad idea, but certainly not a new one. Anyway, the
command line is hidden from all but advanced-level users who don't have a
problem dealing with the syntax."

{ }

A command line tells a computer what you fervently wish it would do, but in
plain text form and strictly following a specific lexicon that may be exclusive to
the program you're running and which varies according to the operating system
of the computer. The computer expects to be addressed precisely, and in its own
terms, literally, with punctuation and spaces all in exactly the right order and
with zero of them left out, thank you very much. Invective doesn't help, and
outbursts of temper are futile. You invoke programs by stating their names and
applying any "switches" or other parameters that the program supports.

They can, for example, run as a background task, open in a new window, or run silently and dump their output to someplace you get to specify—with yet more gibberish typed on the command line. With sophisticated operating systems you can stack so-called "shell" commands together and have the computer execute a list of programs in turn and "pipe" their output to yet other programs with yet other switches and parameters applied. The computer does what you tell it to do, exactly, not necessarily what you want it to do. Graphical user interfaces, which depend on mouse clicks, do the same thing underneath the icons. They simply translate the users' clicks into commands that operate the underlying programs. During development, before those convenient mouse interfaces exist, there is the command line interface and nothing else, relegated to a world of its own, presided over by geeks who, generally, deal with the command shell without complaint.

{ }

"Predictive Analysis considers the user's intent," John bragged, loud, "not just the actual event. It predicts any input activity that results in text entry, so invoking a macro with a mouseclick in a wordprocessor won't fool it." John stuffed his hands in his pockets. "I could make it so anyone running our programs would only need to do a brief demo session, like the one you've done here. After that, the program could predict all of their interaction with any and all of the computers. It could detect attempts to defeat security systems, when they'll enter incorrect data, make disastrous mistakes, and so forth."

"And so forth. And so?"

"The system administrators would know to the minute and second when someone is going to do something that brings the system down. See?" *Thwiiiip*. John straightened a picture, Velcro'd to the cubicle's wall, of his cat Ida sleeping on the sunlit balcony of his apartment.

"See? Sure I see. But believe? Not a bit." *Twitch*. "John, what you're saying is simply not possible. Even if it were, it would consume so much computing power that not even God could afford to use it without taking out a second mortgage on Eden."

"I thought I convinced you with the password."

"Cheap trick. You could have hacked the system beforehand. And for all I know you simulated this whole session." Osgood studied the screen. "Like we do with those infernal benchmarks we show the clients."

John grimaced, pushed the mouse toward his boss. "I don't participate in or approve of that dishonesty and you know it. And as for Predictive Analysis, I don't need fake simulations. However, since you need further proof, hold all three mousebuttons down and roll the mouse toward you. That fast-forwards the program. Moves it ahead in time, so to speak. You're already into early afternoon, so move it into tomorrow and the next day. Monday if you want."

In the next cubicle, Branson typed furiously, grunting in frustration from time to time, guiltily checking over his shoulder.

Osgood hesitated, but kept his hand on the mouse. "This is the present, John, in case you haven't noticed. Can your time machine move my ten o'clock meeting forward? I've still got to make that ten o-clock in real time, not future time, so I really need to go soon. Besides, I have to go to my office and try to repair the security damage you've just caused—because I don't want to spend the whole weekend writing security incident reports, and I do want to see your smiling face around here on Monday. After lunch I've got to start preparing my weekly progress reports, which are due at four o'clock. Real time. Progress reports? Real time? Kramden Company time? You get my drift?"

"So, you're a gambler. How about a bet?" John retrieved his wallet from the his personal effects drawer.

"My reputation for gambling is greatly exaggerated around the office water fountains, but what kind of bet did you have in mind?" Osgood made momentary eye contact and looked away.

"I say my Predictive Analysis program can foretell what you'll type three days from now, on Monday. And I'm willing to bet on it."

"You realize, of course, you're already betting your job that I can repair the security damage without raising any major eyebrows. The odds are not necessarily in your favor on that one." Osgood twitched, held the buttons down and pulled the mouse forward a little. A few more lines of text peeked into the window. He read them, twitched, and scrolled a few more into place.

"I have faith in your abilities to fool security. How about we bet a steak dinner–in addition to my job?"

"Small stakes, no pun intended. Make it more interesting–a week's pay?" Osgood moved the mouse slightly.

"Small stakes, pun intended, but okay." John stored his tattered wallet in the desk drawer and put out his hand to shake.

"*Touché*! Okay, it's a bet." Osgood shook hands quickly, barely making flesh to flesh contact, and would have grabbed the mouse again, but John beat him to it. "What are you doing?"

"I'm sending these predictions to the group LAN's laserprinter, two copies. Lots of pages. See, the program knows you're going to check my login directories to look for my source code."

"I wouldn't do that."

"The program knows you will, so you will. But I've already wiped it clean and it's not there, so you won't find it." John tapped a two-digit filename into a requester and invoked heavy encryption on the save. "That's a safe bet, really, looking for the program after you believe what it can do. I can see that gleam in your eye. You'll understand what I mean on Monday." John caught Osgood's frown. "I've just released the task and expunged the program's processes. It's not running any more. Wait. There's a holdout..." He clicked the mouse and typed some commands. "Object in use? There's supposed to be only one user, and I just released it... Okay, there it goes."

Osgood smoothed his hair, frowned, checked his watch. "You're so confident, even more than usual. How does this predictive business work, anyway? That is, assuming I believed it did work."

Branson rolled his chair over to the bookshelf and took down *Network Protocols*. It might as well have been "*for Dummies*." He could have written it in his sleep. He thumbed the book's index and turned to a random page. Behind him, a command window on his workstation blinked "Saving log files..."

John smiled. "During the training session, I count timing, spacing, and content of what you type. I consider intent–what you want the computer to do–in a highly abstract form with some heavy AI logic. Then I subtract out the AI equivalent of Worley Noise–that's what really makes the software magic happen–and pass the resulting matrix of information through a massive reverse inference engine. Based on your input relative to your intent, the program then learns to predict your keystrokes. The instant you try to impress or confuse, it pegs your profile."

"Profile. Sounds like the load of crap we sold the FBI. But, go on." Osgood studied the text in the maroon window.

"Remember, I was the one who wrote most of the AI routines that we stuck into that crap. My conscience, what's left of it, will never forgive me."

"You wrote what they wanted, all right, yelping all the way about dishonesty, I recall. Loudly. If I hadn't covered for you, we wouldn't be having this conversation." Osgood twitched.

"For which I thank you, I think. Anyway, this program is real science, instead of the pseudo-science they insisted we install in their idiotic nonsense. It conducts an appraisal of available data–honest and objective, without goal-seeking, so it actually works. At the very beginning the program mostly guesses and it's often wrong, but it uses that experience to refine its abilities. It's like a look-ahead buffer that pipes stuff to a 'history.' If you type 'al' and the command 'alias' would be appropriate, my program predicts 'ias' as the next characters you'll type. It then checks whether you've already used the word and in what context. If so, it might predict that you'll invoke command line completion to fill a whole bunch of arguments and switches. That requires a keystroke of its own, you know. It's really at home predicting command lines and source code because they have to follow a strict syntax."

"Quite." Osgood inspected his sleeve.

"So far, it's mostly reverse extrapolation, comparing to a large database of possibilities and refining a profile–not in the FBI's sense of the word. After a time, surprisingly little time, the program becomes much more accurate. All the while it passes its successes and evaluation data to a supervisory inference engine that assigns intent contextually. Again, it learns from mistakes–exponentially, as I said, when you deliberately try to fool it."

"You developed this on Kramden time? Company resources and computers?"

"No. Not one single bit of it, pun intended. I wrote it at home over the last several months. I didn't use anything from here because what we did here was hokum. This is real. I only brought it in today to demonstrate for you."

"I'm honored," Osgood said, cold. He checked his watch.

{ chapter 2 }

Chapter 3 : Start your inference engines

O sgood made a point of looking at the wall clock and checking his watch again. "I trust you had your media tagged at the security desk when you came in–as per security protocol?"

"I sure did," John said. "Seven opticals, inspected and tagged. Takes three whole discs for my oversight Assembler routines that let the program continuously refine itself and improve its performance. It re-compiles some of its own components on the fly. The self-improvement loop can even self-improve itself. I know that's hard to understand, but it works. Maybe too well, I see."

"The deeper you dig, John, the harder it is to get out of a hole." Osgood winked-twitched. "And we're still using company time viewing and discussing this non-company product, for which I don't see any practical application, and which I can assure you Kramden Software has zero interest in purchasing or licensing from you. Is this–hold on a sec." Osgood's cell phone rattled. He retrieved it from his inside coat pocket, smoothed it gently, and popped it open. "Sorry, I've got to take this."

John nodded, set about reordering the windows on the computer screen. "Curious," he said, finding that the Predictive Analysis output window was still open. "I was sure I closed that."

"Osgood," Osgood barked into the phone. He listened for only a second and broke in. "My current situation is not secure for that discussion. I'll call you from my office after my meeting with–er, after my ten o'clock." He closed the phone and put it away, smoothing imaginary wrinkles the phone might have caused in his lapels.

{ }

Kramden Company Security Manual, section 12. Cell phone use within the company building complex is permitted, but cameras and smartphones are not, and Wi-Fi and similar networking devices are prohibited and subject to confiscation. All employees must use camera-less, Wi-Fi-less, email-less cell phones on company property. System Analysts are a permitted exception, provided they use only phones that are issued by the company. The lime green cell phones remain owned by the company, must be surrendered on demand, and are subject to monitoring at all times.

{ }

"Of course I volunteered myself as the first tester."

Osgood twitched, frowned. "Of course."

"So the program was able to learn my profile extremely well while I typed its own source code. After only a little while it could actually predict itself. I just hit the return key now and then to okay the predicted lines. This truly is the program that, like they say, wrote itself."

"Right. It predicted itself. Got it."

John sat down at his terminal. "I sense that you still don't grasp what I've done here, or its potential."

Osgood twitched his face into a threatening look. "Other than wasting company time? We could have taken an early lunch, or hung out in my office and wasted just as much company time without troubling me to come all the way over here for nothing. I've already told you, speaking for the company, that the company has no interest in it. Zero. It is and will remain your personal property. I hope you get as much out of it as you claim it has potential for."

Branson snickered, quiet, caught himself and cleared his throat a couple of times to cover the slip.

"Look at it this way," John said, exuding patience. "This afternoon I'm supposed to finish the flow charting for a security exceptions handler for the intranet systems group. It's a simple program, but it has some complicated security interfacing that's likely to take one or three hours to flowchart and prototype, then a day to code, and then half a week to debug, and then another week to layer into the gooey."

{ }

Gooey, a pronunciation of the initials G.U.I., is programmer shorthand for graphical user interface, the method of operating a computer that entails a deskbound mouse, a screen full of icons and other mouse-friendly structures, not to mention a suitable mousepad adorned with cats, cartoons or portraits of Mr. Spock.

{ }

Osgood brightened. "You did read my memo, then."

John grinned. "I did, for a change, and I've already got the work done. Ta-da! Predictive Analysis fulfills its potential before your very eyes." He leaned over and typed a command. "First it predicts my source code, bugs and all. Then it predicts the debugged version a little further into the future. After that it can even predict what the final source code will look like when everything's all done, all changes made, and with the gooey layer and the cute little user macro language merged."

"What user macro language?" Osgood felt his coat pocket. "You mean more security bots? I can't check the specs from here, but I don't remember anything about a user macro language."

John pressed on, loud, with a broad smile. "I had my Predictive Analysis program process the project all the way to the end product. A program like that wouldn't normally be finished for at least a month, you know," *click-click,* "but this is the end result all finished, debugged, and with everything added to it that hasn't even been requested yet." He typed some commands into a green window. It's compiling and linking now. I see by your scowl that I should reassure you that the Predictive Analysis program itself is not running."

Osgood glared. "It better not be, *Mister* Farmer."

"I'm compiling this from a capture file that I generated with it earlier. Notice the file dates."

"Easily faked, but I'll trust you on that. Okay, go on."

"Finished. Predictive Analysis has turned time forward, so to speak. Instead of wading through the usual development process, we can just send this straight out for beta testing. The end result is ready now, more than a month earlier than normal. Productivity to the max, thanks to Predictive Analysis."

Osgood chuckled nervously. "You expect me to believe that you've just crystal balled the entire development cycle for an esoteric executable?"

"Only the source code, which has to be typed some way, some how, by somebody." John grinned. "It had to be compiled and linked, but I just did that. Predictive Analysis doesn't predict binaries because those are generated, not typed. It does predict the source code, however, and even the compile-link command line. Those can be challenging, as you know. I suppose it could predict interpreted code, but I haven't tried it."

"Did you get this Predict-o-thing-o program from a little green alien on your last trip to Mars?"

"Gotta watch out for those anal probes, but no, I haven't visited Mars. Yet." John momentarily put a comforting hand on Osgood's shoulder. "I have been to Ohio. Doesn't that count for pretty much the same thing? Oz, It took me a long time to believe it, too, if that's any consolation." He opened a louvered door in the desk, popped an orange floppy disk, emblazoned with the Kramden Company logo, out of the computer, and handed it to Osgood. "I don't want to send this through the office email because it doesn't exist yet. Don't know what that would do to the future."

"Pfffft! The future. Exist or not, who's to say you didn't write this in advance?"

John pointed to the screen, where he had opened an emailed document. "Your go-ahead-and-code memo only came in this morning. I couldn't have known what would even be required until today, much less develop the whole thing, even laying in the user interface, in only a couple of hours. I'm good, but not that good."

Osgood was looking over the wall at Branson's screen and didn't see John's wink. Odd. Very odd. He turned back to John. "So you sniffed the specs from the company grapevine–maybe with the help of some connection you've got in the intranets section? What's her name down there? Erica something. Or was it Eric? Used to work in this section? Left to do consulting, and even Kramden brought him in, or was it her, as a contractor for some Security hardware thing or other. Or maybe you tapped into somebody's memo files on the network. You have no trouble accessing all the passwords, it seems."

"Nope. I could have done that, but I didn't have to, and I didn't. You know I never lie, to you or anyone else, not even when fibs would save me from a lot of trouble. And I'm not lying to you now." John leaned in and held eye contact. "I promise you, the executable on that flex did not exist before I compiled it just now. Nor the source, which I've just cc'd to your email box for checking. None of it existed before this morning, shortly before you came in."

"Let me see that." Osgood tapped the back of John's chair and sat down at the terminal as John moved out of the way. "This looks like the intranet thing, all right, but–It's all wrong." He stopped, pointed, twisted around to look John in the eye. "This wide-area option wasn't in the specification."

John shrugged. "Remember you're looking at it in the future after considerable development has taken place. Someone has probably asked for that additional cloud feature by the time this code would exist."

"Wide area lookup's no small feat or feature. Can you consult your electronic crystal ball and tell me who's footing the bill for programming and testing it? And who gets the invoices for the maintenance updates? Wait, how about something more useful. The winning numbers for the Oregon lottery? The outcome of the Kentucky Derby? Monday's closing stock markets? Future information like that could make some real money. Maybe even for somebody besides Kramden."

Branson cleared his throat, scribbling notes frantically, tapping the Return key from time to time.

"Do you want to make another risky wager about the inclusion of that wide-area feature?"

"Gladly." Osgood slipped the floppy disk into his shirt pocket behind his Mont Blanc pen and smoothed the pocket. Rarely taken out, except for ceremonial occasions and at Nineteenth Floor meetings, the fountain pen had a nearly full belly of ink, and its point was like new. For plebeian scribblings, Osgood kept a Parker ballpoint pen and a mechanical pencil in his inside coat pocket. Particularly useful if someone wanted to borrow a pen.

"A hundred bucks?"

"Why not?"

"Done."

Osgood checked his watch, winked at John, whispered, "Sorry about this, but you brought it on yourself." He clicked the "Record" button on his portable voice recorder–not much bigger than his pen–cleared his throat, and spoke loudly. "Now, I've really got to hurry to get to my ten o'clock. Uh, I'll send you a memo on this, but I need to make it quite clear verbally, also. Provably so, in case Security insists on knowing." Osgood peered over the partition into the adjacent cubicle. "Mister...?"

"Branson," wheezed Branson, furiously typing at his terminal. "Jerry. I'm the networking specialist in this section."

"Oh yes, I think I remember hiring you, Bramson. You're hearing this, aren't you?" Osgood held his voice recorder half an arm's length forward. "I want you to stand witness to my verbal instructions to your cube neighbor, Mister Farmer. I'm setting this thing to 'Record...' beginning... now." Osgood twitched, hesitated only a second, and went on. "Take note of the time: It's 0948. I'm formally advising Mr. Farmer to immediately and completely expunge his personal property, which is an executable program along with its source code and all of its generated and original resources from Kramden Company systems. He tells me he's done that, as of now."

"Right," said John, glancing at the ceiling. "I did that minutes ago."

Branson stood up. "Then he did," he said, assertive, taking Osgood aback. "John is our group role model. We all trust him implicitly and you can, too." Branson didn't much look the part of the brash persona he projected. Tall, round shouldered, and excruciatingly skinny, his gaunt figure peered out through thick-lensed glasses that competed for space at his eyes with a bushy red monobrow.

Osgood turned to John. "Mister Farmer, that means completely and immediately, and never run your program here again. Ever. And definitely remove your personal property optical discs from the building when you leave today." He clicked the "Rec" button off.

"Right, sir. As you wish, sir." John saluted smartly.

"I could send Security over to inspect," Osgood warned, mostly to Branson.

"No need." John exchanged sheepish looks with Branson.

"I'll have Miss Mumblebody, I mean Barb, transcribe this and send it to you in an official paper memo."

"No need," John said. "But feel free put it in some official file if you need to." He sat down and looked up at Osgood. "Your point is made. Dog and pony show finished. I apologize for inconveniencing you. See you at lunch."

"It is an interesting idea, I'll give you that. Roddenbury and Serling would love it. Might make a great movie someday. Go well with hot buttered popcorn. Or maybe commercials."

"Really, I get it now," John said, quietly for once, "it's just too hard to believe, and way too scary. I can see that now. Should have left it at home. I don't know what I was thinking." He sighed. "It's really a good thing you don't understand it, because Kramden Software could not be trusted with such a thing. I can suddenly see the full potential for abusing it, and it isn't pretty, though I'm afraid it's already too late to stop." John looked up, sighed. "Oz, I've stored the output files for our little bet, and I'll just shred my optical discs. No need bothering to take them home, since the program runs on my home system around the clock. It will probably be able to refine itself at least to this level or maybe even further by the time you're ready to believe it."

"Oh, I'm not going to want it. Or believe it, either. And I'll expect your productivity here not to reflect any development time you spend on it."

"Naturally." John smiled, sitting down at the terminal as Osgood peered around, twitching violently. "rm /tmp/myprog/*..." he typed. "There! All gone."

"Except for the network caches, server histories, and security tracking," Osgood reminded.

"Bingo," Branson muttered, jubilant, and typed furiously at his keyboard.

"I'll try to delete the histories when I get back to my office–before Security notices them. Save us both some hassle. Now, about that bet?" Osgood frowned. "You know Kramden Company policy is--"

"Bets off? Sure, no prob."

"Definitely all bets off." Osgood looked pointedly at his watch. "I'll let you get back to your work. Submit the preliminary source for that intranet program to CVS so they can start chasing their usual approvals. Go ahead and email a link to the executable to Maryanne Anderson in QA so they can start checking it, and copy Barb on everything."

{ }

In Kramden corporate-speak, QA is the standard sobriquet for that odd group of powerful, important nerds who try to break software before the customers get the chance. Often mispronounced with extra stress on the first syllable in "assurance," the Quality ASSurance group has its own budgets, its own protocols, its own politics, and its own mission: find faults in other people's work. With a vengeance. It's one of many places in Kramden's vast political system where angering someone powerful can be exceedingly dangerous.

When you send a product to QA, its development cycle is complete, and it's ready to face the onslaught of mere humans—which QA's minions pretend to be. However, QA never sees the source code—those umpty-thousand k-lines of Compuspeak that make the computer do its thing. That's because QA's job is to find faults, not fix them.

In software development, the often voluminous source code has a life of its own, especially after a project moves to QA. The k-lines get "compiled" to create "binaries," the latter being the actual executable programs that run on the customers' computers or servers, on their PDA's, their smartphones, gameboxes, missile defense systems or microwave ovens. To make changes and create a new version of a program, programmers re-edit and re-compile the source code, adding or altering as necessary.

In large companies, especially, where many people might be involved in developing a single project, the Powers That Be impose strict protocols for accessing, altering, updating or adding to the company's source code files, which are considered extremely valuable intellectual properties. Achieved at great cost over many k-lines and numerous man years, these must be guarded like furs and jewels from inadvertent deletion, corruption, loss or theft in spite of any and all onslaughts from nature, employees–well-meaning or otherwise–or from hackers bent on doing evil. The source code files must be protected like the crown jewels from unwelcome, prying eyes, and from accidental or intentional corruption by the addition of sloppy code, yet must remain accessible for updating and additions.

The corporate Fort Knox for such vaporous electronic treasure is "source code control," where specialized servers and software collectively called "CVS" guard the goodies as jealous husbands would guard a harem. Committing something to CVS is like recognizing its value and locking it in a vault, preserving it for posterity whether or not posterity is interested. The painstakingly configured CVS servers–automated bots, in a sense–strictly proscribe who gets to look at anything or change it. They log all accesses, track all alterations, deletions or additions, and maintain "snapshots" of data so that virtually any activity can be undone to any previous state if need be–and if sufficiently authoritative and verifiably-sourced memos get sent to the right place by the right people, or at least by the right bots. The server bots also maintain multitudinous, on-site and off-site redundant backups of absolutely everything, just in case.

John cocked his eyes at his boss quizzically. "This is going to be interesting. See, the source code exists right now as it would in the future, after QA has already seen it."

"I don't believe that and even if I did, I don't see how it matters."

"Oh-oh," muttered Branson, hunched over his workstation. He looked around and hurried to turn his chair sidewise to obscure his monitor from view over the cubicle wall.

Osgood peered into Branson's cubicle. "Excuse me?"

"Sorry, just talking to myself over here." Branson cleared his throat, nervous. "Don't mean to disturb you."

"This is extremely dangerous. I can feel the vibes. Strong." John stared at the screen, his hands poised over the keyboard. "The point is, if I send it to QA now... and particularly if I commit it to CVS, where it shouldn't be until after it would have already been logged in and all the change orders recorded and backed up, and–"

"Well?" Osgood tapped his watch.

"Oh what the hell, I'll just send it. This is bad. I just know it." John tapped the Return key.

Osgood glared at his watch and edged toward the corridor. "You really do think you're messing with the future."

"I know I am, and right now it's scaring me more than it ever has. Much more than you understand right now. We are—that's us, here in the present—we're not supposed to change the course of the events of the future, on account of the far-reaching consequences our changes would have in the future, which becomes the past that we're in as soon as we change anything—that quantum thing, you know, with the poor doomed pussycat. Observing something changes it just by the fact that it's being observed. Well, you know what I mean, but it's hard to say in words."

"Hogwash. That's the word for it and it's not at all hard to say. I'd be more descriptive, but company protocol prohibits further utterance. Anyway, much as I'd love to, I don't have time to debate science fiction with you at the moment." Osgood stormed off.

"See ya," John said to himself, and immersed himself in his terminal. "Science fiction, indeed," he muttered. "This is no fiction."

Branson hid a maroon window under his command screen. He peeked over the cubicle wall. "Good grief, John. I mean, 'Mister Farmer.' What in the world, to use the term lightly, was that all about?"

"Oz," John said simply. "He's looking out for protecting his ass in case Security tries to pin something on him. Way sorry about the soap opera. Me being personal friends with him outside of the office is what brought on most of the drama. He insists on thinking he has to document that he's treating me like everyone else, so everyone else won't complain that he's not treating me like everyone else."

"Okay." Branson chuckled. "As if anybody is permitted to care. Or to object."

"But he doesn't hang out at lunch with everyone else or go to movies with them, or visit exotic tourist traps and such, or even make extended eye contact, so what's to prove?"

"Sounded more like he was intent on establishing non-company ownership of your program. That's probably to your benefit, especially for patent protection purposes. Keep Kramden from claiming royalties, or maybe from preventing you from selling to someone else." He shielded his monitor from John's view by standing in front of it. "I overheard some of what you described, and I think he did you a big favor by doing that. Your program sounds like it has big time patentability, like venture capitalizers would eat it up and shell out great sums to develop it further." Branson reached over and clicked his mouse uselessly. "Compiling." He stood in front of his monitor, hiding a sliver of the maroon window that peeked out. "So, does it work? I mean, predicting the future?"

"Works too well," John said. "I've learned that much about it just now. Oooo, I'm getting really bad vibes all of a sudden. Like just before a major storm."

"Sounded interesting. What I heard of what it can do. It's finished?"

"Almost. Just need to tidy up some debug code and spruce up the cosmetics. Add some basic documentation. Trap a few input errors, just in case. I'm not going to do anything else with it, though." John extracted an optical disc from his personal drawer, broke it in half and tossed the halves into the trash bin with the six others he'd already destroyed. "Easier than getting them out through Security," he explained to Branson's amazed gaze. "I have them backed up at home, anyway."

"Well, that was all very entertaining, but I hope you'll be so kind as to give us all plenty of notice next time before you encourage an Osgood visit. Then we can hold a module development meeting in the conference room, or all go take wicked dumps, or maybe go lock ourselves in the elevator and report it broken. Or something."

"Sorry. I decided to test the program on my project and I wanted Oz to know how I did it and see the program in action. I kept it in my private directories so Security couldn't claim it. The demo didn't work too well, I guess. But everything's fine, now." John sat down and Branson did, too. "I hope. Really, it was a spur of the moment inspiration."

"I hope it doesn't spur-of-the-moment you out of here. Osgood wouldn't have responded at all to anyone else, you know." Branson checked over his shoulder, clicked the maroon window to the front and covered it with a command window. He typed carefully at the terminal's prompt, checked over his shoulder again, and hit "Return."

"> File saved," the computer responded.

"Probably not, but sometimes he surprises even me."

{ chapter 3 }

Chapter 4 : Quality assurances

*T*uesday morning.

"Morning, John. Have a seat. Your intranet program from last week? You were copied on those emails from QA?" Osgood squeaked forward in his chair and propped his elbow on his desk, nervousness obvious, diddling the Control key on his keyboard as he talked. "It's unusually complimentary."

John fidgeted, sat down. "I read the whole thread. Did they change their meds? Take up transcendental meditation over the weekend? All go off the rag at one time?"

"Such high praise is most uncharacteristic of them, true." Osgood's mammoth computer terminal had a single "$>" command prompt in the top left corner of its teal-colored screen. "They rave about your inline docs, too. And documentation is not altogether usual for you, I need not point out."

"That hasn't been my strong point one or three times." John smiled. "Truth be told."

"Truth told bluntly, as usual" Osgood said. "But that's not my point."

"Then what is? Bluntly, even."

"Bluntly, this is Tuesday."

"All day," John said, cheerful. "Especially if it rains. We're still on for lunch, I assume?"

"Sure. Your choice, your treat. You're going to make me say it, then? Fine. I kept a log of my keystrokes yesterday, to compare them with your ridiculous prediction thing."

"Right. Oz, we canceled the bets, remember, so you don't owe me your salary this week," John smiled, gracious. "Too bad. I could use a new Beemer. Is there a bike rack option on those?"

"Saab. Just as nicely built and high performance, too. Air bags all over the place. Great for the freeway and other demolition derbies. I wrecked one on the Autobahn last year and lived to tell about it. Barely a scratch. I know we canceled the bet, but you can call me curious, I still want to know whether your prediction thing worked."

"It worked perfectly, I predict, Mister Curious."

"And the proof, Mister Smarty?" Osgood held out his hand, palm up, and wiggled his fingers.

"I thought you'd already seen it. I sent you the printout through office mail Friday. Handled only by the most qualified nincompoops in the Kramden Company inter-departmental mail pool. It should have been in your mailbox Friday." John stuck his hands in his pockets, slumped in his chair, crossed his legs. "Actual paper, sealed and certified so there's not even the slightest question about it being faked."

"Well it isn't here. Where... Ohhh, the snail box. We're so electronic around here it's easy to forget paper even exists." Osgood leafed through a tall, neat stack of envelopes on the far corner of his desk. Each packet bore orange-inked rubber stamped notices: "TRADE SECRETS", "RUSH!", "SIGNATURE REQUIRED, PROPRIETARY INFORMATION, TOP SECURITY," plus whole paragraphs of curt, bold-print all-cap threats–legalese forbidding use and abuse of the contents and promising heinous penalties for disobedience. "Here it is. Nice of people to sign my name for stuff and not even bring it to my attention. I'll definitely take that up with Security at this afternoon's meeting. Let's see..."

As Osgood tore open the envelope, John glanced at Osgood's screen. "Nada?"

"That's right. I typed absolutely nothing from here all day yesterday. Signed into my remote-enabled account early in the morning from my laptop at home to read email, and when I got to the office I ended up in meetings on the nineteenth floor anyway, so no activity needed. This terminal stayed locked all day. Let's see your predict-o whizz-o program analyze that."

"Better make sure you're sitting down when you read that transcript, then. But first observe that the trusty interdepartmental post office dweebs have stamped Friday's date onto every possible seam of the envelope. Security Level

Three, named recipient only–even though your intern signed for it. Proves it hasn't been tampered with. It hasn't been opened, and was definitely in their capable hands–See the stamp? On Friday."

Osgood opened the document, scoffed, ruffled, boiled.

John stood up and peered over Osgood's shoulder. "You typed these first few commands at this terminal–sign on, then attempt to find Predictive Analysis in the system–I really did expunge it, like I said, which is why you couldn't find it. You looked around for my source code–here and here, see?–and didn't find it in the sandbox listing, so you checked some locations on the group network for it–my section, and then Branson's terminal for some reason. He was unceremoniously banned from the building and fired Friday afternoon, I'm sure you recall. And then you signed off. Exactly as my program predicted on Friday. Exactly."

"OzG&20$0+0mro|o–that's my new password! As of when I changed it yet again yesterday morning. How the hell? Here's my whole email session, too. It's all here! Every word. How the... I did all this yesterday from my home over a secure connection that's encrypted beyond belief. And you stored this log–Friday? How could it–?"

John shrugged. "Once the program establishes your profile, it doesn't matter where you type from, only that it's you causing the input on the company's system. Getting through the encryption–that's beyond what I expected, but the predictive algorithm calculates a probability factor and weighs the result against your dynamically refined profile. It doesn't matter what gets transmitted over the connection, I guess, only what you type, and what you typed was unencrypted. See, here's where you tried to fool it again. That's how it became so accurate with you so quickly. When you're typing from remote locations that only means it can't further refine its profile, but it's still working on you, no matter where you are. Notice it even predicted the backspaces."

"This is uncanny!"

"Yes, canny it is not." John grinned. "It's a good thing we called off that bet, because I'd definitely spend your money on something frivolous and dangerous and probably not even tell you her name."

"This is impossible," Osgood said. "If you didn't hack the system to stage this—and I'm convinced you didn't or you'd already be joining Batson waving bye-bye from the exit gate—then how did you get this trick to work?"

"You're quite right. It is impossible. But really, once I got the idea and sketched out the program flow, all I had to do was start it on its way. The self-improvement and learning loop was the most important component. Once I turned that loose and set the program predicting itself, it developed to this advanced level mostly on its own. I've tried to follow the logic in the way it revised itself—and I'm pretty good with Assembler, as you know. No way I could figure it out. I'd call it brilliant but it's too creepy. It's way creepy, in fact. Especially the source code, complete with comments that include my usual misspellings."

"No kidding." Osgood mopped his brow and stowed the handkerchief in a desk drawer, retrieving a fresh hank from the drawer below.

John kept going. "It does exactly what you'd expect. Stores hashed lists, compares elements, tables of weighted probabilities. But I couldn't follow how it manages to extrapolate its predictions, even from reading its source code that I somehow wrote. Frankly, after looking through these logs, I'm beginning to be afraid of what havoc it might cause—if it hasn't already."

"Oh, man, run it. Run it by all means. You could predict stock closings, the dog races, blackjack, politics—"

"The next war, the end of the world, the scores from next week's company volleyball tournament? I thought about this all weekend while I was climbing. Kind of a 'What hath John wrought' thing. How 'bout if it predicts the Intranets Group to lose at Volleyball? Why should we even play, then? We just forfeit the game and do other things instead. I could climb Runningtree Ridge again. I know that's a frivolous example, but it brings home the problem. Predictive Analysis is way too dangerous." John sighed. "The best thing about the future is that we *don't* know what it holds—except of course in a general way, based on what we do in the present to screw it up."

"True that."

"If we knew exactly what to expect and couldn't change any of it, we couldn't resist trying to change it anyway, and we'd go nuts."

"Nuts-ER," Osgood corrected. He lowered his voice. "What else has it done? You've been running this at your apartment for a while, haven't you? We're still on company time, here, but it's close enough to lunch time, so we won't bother about that." He cast a glance at his office door. "Keep it down, so Barb won't hear us."

John winked. "Got it. I've left it running on my home system so it could refine itself or any part of itself. Right now I'm tempted to rush home and shut it down, but my gut tells me it's already too late for that. My home system doesn't have the computing power of the company's distributed network, so I designed it to devote most of its time doing itself to itself, trying to improve its own code. When I loaded it here, I forgot to change the priority file that turns that function off, so it improved itself immensely in just a few minutes. It even upped its version number a few places."

"Wonderful."

"But I really should have disabled the self-improvement module when I loaded it here. That has made it much more powerful and far more scary."

"Yes."

"It was so sweet, though," John apologized. "The minute I opened the program it used itself to look into the future at its source code some time from now, copied those routines and recompiled portions of itself. With Kramden's huge computing power behind it the whole process took seconds, and the difference really boggles the mind. Even mine."

"No kidding." Osgood looked shocked. "Not that I'd ever want to, but–I mean, it's not in the Kramden Company's interest to–I mean, we are still on company time, here, but what do you plan to do with your program? Note I said 'your' since the whole program is entirely your creation and none of it belongs to the company."

"I don't know," John said, shrugged. "A part of me wants to let it run to see what it'll do, and another part of me wants to rip it out of its socket and destroy the source forever and then stomp the computer it's using into tiny little bits– and particularly to forget I ever came up with the idea. Other than frivolous testing, so far I've only ever invoked it for serious to develop the intranet program that QA is raving about. And despite their raves, I'm still sensing bad vibes to come from this episode. Way bad."

"I'm not a 'vibes' person, but that's a safe bet. Those cuckoos are loose cannon, and that's before they encounter your predict-o-thing-o."

"Exactly why I wouldn't dare use it like that again. Shouldn't have done so to begin with. It's dangerous revising the history of the future's past."

"History of the future past. What a concept. But you've really already done that, and as you say, the vibes are not good."

A delicate, timid wrist slipped through the open door and knocked, knuckles barely stirring the air.

"Come on in!" Osgood shouted, snugged his perfectly knotted, Italian silk tie. Tuesday the cool-gray. Pale yellow on Wednesdays, barring meetings on Nineteenth Floor. Thursdays and all occasions on Nineteen: navy.

"These came over the fax for you just now." Barb Scott, Osgood's lithe, super-intelligent intern from nearby Wendover Technical College, held out a neat laserprint. A snappy dresser, she wore a dark, well fitted skirt with a downplayed white blouse that showed off her bust and a rakish kerchief left untied. Balancing on one foot like a skilled ballerina, she deftly propped her heel on the heavy door to prevent it from closing behind her. "Sorry, I forgot you were in a meeting."

"Thanks, Barb," Osgood said. "No problem, this is just a quick bull session before we leave for lunch." He took the papers, lowered his chin, elevated his eyebrows, speed-read the top document. "Close the door behind you, will you. I see from this fax that our bull session's suddenly over and we need to address some issues. He waited for the door to snap closed before looking back at the faxes, passing the top page to John. "Oh, crap. Your intranet program's already gone out with that wide-area feature in it, and I'm just now getting this memo from Beakman asking that it be added and authorizing funding for it. This is mixed up."

{ }

The unflattering sobriquet "Beakman" refers to L. Harry Smith, almighty high exalted boss-in-chief of the corporate intranets group. His powerful entity manages the complex networks that link the company's myriad computers to departmental heads, to security oversight panels, to corporate mainframes, to remote offices, to satellite feeds, to Realms Beyond the Known Universe Itself, and to each other, all with layers on layers of security checks. His nickname has nothing to do with beaks, but his physiognomy does.

{ }

John shuddered. "Bad, bad, bad. I sensed this would be a problem. The vibes are always right. You know Beakman better than I do. What's going on? Honestly, I don't know what to do, if anything."

"I don't suppose you believe in any gods."

"Sure do."

Osgood dropped a document into the shredder. "Different issue," he explained to John's quizzical look. "It was mostly a rhetorical question, but I never would have figured you for a religion anybody could put a name on."

"You said god, not religion."

"Semantics. Well, your predicter thing isn't God, and you're not, and I'm not, and if I were I wouldn't work here and neither would you. But I really doubt either of us wants to be in charge of Time Itself–you know, with the finger quotes and the capital letters, the echo chamber effect and all that."

John chuckled, grimaced. "I have no interest in doing the Time Lord thing. I'd get claustrophobic in those British phone boxes."

"Beakman is no laughing matter. Once someone in QA yanks his chain, he'll raise a stink that not even a Kryptonian phone box could contain. We're cooked if we don't do something. But what?" Osgood leaned far back in his chair and squinted. "You know, it's awfully tempting to put your program's abilities to use on this problem. Suppose we let it–"

John interrupted. "Suppose we don't."

"Well, you're probably right. The thing's caused way too much trouble already, most likely. But can't you reverse the process some way? Did you build in an undo? Unwrite all the memos? Uncode the source? Uncompile? Invert the reversion or something? De-construct? It always works in the movies."

John grinned. "Reverse polarity on the polarity generator, toss in some extra di-librium crystals, and short out the bindlesnorf engine? Grab the girl in the blue tights and make way to the phone box just in the nick of Time-time-time-time? Hah! Guess you've noticed this isn't the movies. Nor Who. Nor Oz. No pun intended. Nor fuzzy little busybody dogs with a mouthful of curtain."

"Nor Kansas, thank all gods that may be." Osgood, a native of Topeka, holder of an undergraduate degree from the University of Southern Kansas, took his advanced degrees from places as far removed from Kansas as possible. On purpose. "I'm getting a bad feeling about this. There's no way Beakman could poke around and find something, is there? You're sure no part of that predicter program's still lurking in the system?"

John said nothing. Frowned.

"Well, is it?"

"I shut it down last week. Three clicks, remember? But it instantiates some things–subtasks that it sets up on its own when it recompiles itself. Those take a minute to clear themselves and relinquish their resources. Those might have been visible to the network security bots for a time. Not very long, but maybe. Wait a a minute. I forgot about Branson. The tinkering he did could have kept some task alive or left a trail that you didn't know about and therefore couldn't expunge. As far as running, no, but portions of it might still lurk on account of Branson. I'm fairly certain he was tinkering around trying to hack into the source code right in front of me. He's gone, and the weekly system reset would have eliminated any lurking tasks at three or five o'clock Sunday morning. Unless the backup bots... Well, in all probability, it's probably gone. But possibly not all of it, traceably or not."

Barb knocked, pushed open the door, grinned and handed Osgood a sheaf of memos. "More faxes, mega rush," she said, hastened out.

"Thanks, Barb." Osgood thumbed through the stack. "Beakman again," he reported. "I don't like that word 'probably' at all. Components might have been backed up to the remote server by the automated system before I intervened Friday, or something Badson left behind–scary thought. Did you forget about that? They'd be restored by the backup scripts and–I don't even want to think it." Osgood frowned, turned to his terminal. "Don't look for a sec." He logged in as global administrator and typed some commands, fast. "I'll redirect task status for the whole network and email it to you. This listing will have entries in it that you are not to discuss with anyone else, ever, or even let on to anyone that you know they exist. If you don't know what it is, don't ask, and don't admit you've seen it, okay?

"Right. My mips are sealed."

"I'm sending you a list of everything their securebots can see. Don't ask me how I can do this. I just can. John, check this very carefully, please. We must be sure there's no trace of your predicter thing in the system, especially not visible to Security, even if it's dormant, or orphaned, which we hope it is. Protect our collective butt, so we can tell the truth if we have to and not get caught doing it."

"My program's not a virus," John said, defensive. "It never tries to obtain information about the system–that would bring down a security bot for sure–and it never tries to propagate itself. I gave it only the security passes it needed to run my demo only within my allotted resources."

Osgood twitched, turned and smiled. "You don't know about the *hidden* security checks. I wrote those myself. That reminds me–" Osgood typed some more commands. "I'll run a check on execute passes, too." Osgood held up his hand, flicked the button on the intercom with the other. "Go ahead," he said toward the phone. "Osgood, non-secure."

"Non secure's fine," a gravelly voice growled. "Fortman here."

{ }

Around the office, Fred Fortman, often referred to in his absence as "Fart Man," runs the networks. He has power over who gets a terminal and how it hooks up to what networks and with what technology, and which security level someone gets, zero to ninety. Only he enjoys level ninety. Unless massive numbers of memos change hands, Fortman never grants more than security level two. At level one, the security is so tight a screenblanker never unblanks.

John has security level ten, two above most of the other programmers, owing to his work for the intranets group. When posting source code snippets he can temporarily gain level fifty with appropriate approvals. Osgood's status in the hierarchy grants the systems analyst security level eighty, but his unique position as author of the security programs gives him far greater access than Fortman or anyone else knows about or even knows the existence of.

{ }

"What the hell's going on over there?" Fortman demanded.

"I'm checking on it now." Osgood puzzled, tapped keys frantically. "Must be an errant compile in progress. I'll take care of it."

"ETA? Noonish? Meaning less than ten minutes from now?" It was more of a threat than a query.

"Or sooner," Osgood promised. He frowned sidewise at John.

"Now, about that sniffer the suits want," Fortman growled. "Do they need–"

"Non secure," Osgood reminded, cut him off. "I'll give you a call after lunch. Two-ish. If I'm not too busy."

"Right." Fortman hung up.

"Uh-oh." John sighed, heavy. "I feel lunch and appetite being ruined, even as we speak."

Osgood tossed the phone into its cradle. "Uh-oh is right. Fart Man's already noticed something. Fortunately, he doesn't know what and doesn't have time before he leaves for lunch to figure it out."

"Whew. Well, really, the three clicks Friday should have done it–you know how obsessive I am about cleaning up on exit. I just couldn't shake the uneasy feeling. Still haven't. The vibes, you know."

"We can't be too careful, especially now that we know Fart Man is poking around. Hmmm. I see disk space is super tight on the section's main server. That's probably what's giving Fart Man a hard-on. This is way out of line. You don't suppose–?"

"The prediction program doesn't store huge files. Check the memory pools. That's where it would eat resources if it's still dormant. Unless it's storing–nah, never mind."

"I'll grep the task list to be sure."

{ }

In computerspeak, grep is a time-honored technique for finding needle-sized treasure–some odd combination of letters, punctuation and numbers–within the haystack-sized alphabet-soup that constitutes computer file storage. Grep (meaning "get regular expression") enables a complex syntax that permits finding occurrences of a string of characters–word, phrase, or computer gibberish–using or not using wildcards, and-slash-or within x number of characters of something else, containing any combination of specified variants, *et cetera ad infinitum.* Even a minor invocation entails a command line that looks like Klingons took over the screen.

{ }

Osgood momentarily stopped for thought a couple of times as he precisely keyed a complex command. He smacked the Return key, pored through the weird lists that snaked up the screen, tapping the space bar to display screens of text one at a time. "Normal so far," he reported. *Tap.* "Normal." *Tap.* "Norm– wait a minute. Huge memory allocations in your section. Super huge. Enough to cause major paging, in fact. Maybe even enough paging to account for the whole disk usage thing. Looks like Brackston's compiling something huge. Cranston, was it? Cube next to yours? G-1853."

"Branson," John said. "His name should be burned into your memory after all the hooplah and the attempted theft. I'm betting you won't be done sending memos on that episode for another week. Anyway, if he's compiling at all it's a security breach from outside the firewalls. He was barred from the property for trying to steal my program. Besides, a large compile was most unusual for him, he only wrote tiny modules of networking code. Never did a major build."

"Well, his account is doing a major compile-link now, for sure, and it was closed days ago." Osgood typed some commands into another window, turned back to his command window. "Other than that, there's very little going on, a fact I should bring up at tomorrow morning's productivity briefing."

John mused. "Branson from outside? There's something very odd going on there, probably something Security needs to know about, but definitely something we don't dare tell them. I'm amazed you're not steaming, yourself." He shrugged. "But, unless Branson's succeeded in getting remote access and managed to steal the executable before I closed it, Predictive Analysis is not running. The massive hash tables and reverse inference logic eat memory for lunch. Damn, damn, mega-damn. I never should have given it the ability to recompile itself."

"Don't look a sec." Osgood shielded the screen from view as he typed some commands. "Branson's terminal has been extremely busy for an hour this morning, and he's over his disk quota by thousands of percent. I suspect–well, you know."

John shrugged. "How would he have access at all, much less for exceeding his quotas by that much? And how is he getting in from outside, unless he somehow broke in and is hiding in one of the equipment closets?"

"How indeed. I don't see how we can answer that without setting off a massive Security check, which we don't want to do."

{ chapter 4 }

Chapter 5 : The errant program does not err

"I'll do some more checking on that right now." Osgood typed a few characters on his keyboard with a determined grin over his shoulder at John. "You don't see me doing this. I can invoke some bots that no one knows about but me. I don't dare run them from this terminal, though. Security tracks this one big time. So I issue a seemingly innocuous command with a switch that launches a background task that... well, you don't want to know."

"Fart Man's dreaded crawlers," John said. "Does anybody around here know who is doing what to whom any more? Or how? Or why?"

"Not any more. Not in a long time, in fact."

{ }

A "crawler" is a bit of robotic software that snoops around networks to find things. Namely, it tries to find things that people might wish were *not* findable, like invocations of forbidden programs or, in Kramden Software's case, failures to compile any programs–indications of no work being done. Crawlers can look into caches of data that even sophisticated users might be unable to delete fast enough to evade scrutiny. Given the proper permissions, they can wreak havoc, either by altering what they find or by reporting it to entities, human or otherwise, charged with scrutiny of such things.

{ }

Osgood studied a black window full of green text. "Not since– Wait a minute. John, your Predictive Thing recompiles itself often?"

"On the fly, all the time," John bragged. "That's how it refines its accuracy so fast. But it only does the modules it needs, and it can recompile even while some of its threads are still executing."

"Of course."

"Appending and reordering rule-based logic took too long, even with massive hash tables, so I had to do something to compensate."

"So, I should check for calls to the compilers?"

"Won't matter," John said. "It writes its own code using a pseudo language that I created. I embedded a scalar compiler for it to use on itself. It even adjusts its recompiles according to the bandwidth that's available on the system it's running on."

Osgood nodded, nodded, and nodded again. "Brilliant, exactly what I've come to expect of you—not just high-performance but system-considerate."

John smirked. "I always aim to please."

Osgood slumped at his computer. "But in this case, that's a problem. You wrote a compiler into the program, so now there's no way to simply disable the program's access to a compiler resource. And no way to track its use."

"I see that, now," John said. "I had to make it do itself because I was having trouble following the logic. It's super complex code."

"Safe bet on that. Well, something is hogging the networks' resources, and the non-existent Banson is doing something that's several thousand percent of his normal daily output. This makes me very suspicious. And mad. But I don't dare do much more poking around because Fart Man's unleashing his bots—and if El Loco Predict-o isn't running in the system, what is?" Osgood didn't wait for an answer. "Hmmm. I'm redirecting all output from Branson's processes to me. You don't know how I'm doing this, or that I can do it. Better set a background task to do the job, in case Fart Man's crawlers come by. There. Now Branton won't get anything but carriage returns, wherever he is."

"Good idea. Tacky, but good. At least we can see what he's doing, if he's doing anything. How in the world is he getting in from outside, anyway? I'm betting he put something in the network code to let himself in."

"Hmmm, safe bet. Well, I've got some bots that'll shut that down in a jiffy." Osgood typed some commands and smacked the Return key. "So much for unauthorized access from outside the firewalls."

A minute. Two.

"Can't wait any longer. Fart Man just logged on. You don't know how I know that, okay? Time for desperate measures. You are not seeing what I'm doing."

"I see nuttink," John quipped, looked away momentarily. "Holy crap! A system-wide reset? You can do that?"

Osgood smiled, wicked. "No, I can't. At least officially I can't. No one can, and like I said you did *not* see me do it, either. Remember I *wrote* the crawlers that Fart Man just invoked."

"Ohhh. Now I see. Though of course I still know nothing."

Osgood twitched. "The best part is, Security's reports will say Fart Man did it, and for all he knows he did, although he'll undoubtedly convince himself someone else did."

"Mean. Dangerous, too. Remind me not to ever piss you off."

"What else could I do?" Osgood picked up the phone, counted down from three on his fingers, and punched 45299, fast. "Osgood here, not secure again."

"Still? You know we need secure to t–" The gravelly voice blustered. "What is it, now?"

"The network is being reset. At least our corner of it is. All servers."

"It is?"

"It is." Osgood grinned at John, frowned into the phone, raised his voice a notch. "It is, and you know it is, and I know you know it, because I can hear your terminals beeping through the phone."

"Looks like whatever you guys had that was causing the problem brought the whole thing down, eh?" Fortman blustered.

"Eh no? Looks more like you caused it," Osgood accused, louder.

"Well I didn't."

"That's not what the little blue window on my screen says."

"I– but how is this possible?"

"Doesn't much matter, THIS time, since most everybody's winding down for lunch" Osgood returned his voice to its measured, even-toned normal. Smooth. "We would have had to request a reboot on our end anyway, to kill whatever it was that was running amuck, but I'm *supposed* to get a few minutes notice before you invoke a reset. You know that, don't you? We're running a business

here, not a computer kindergarten? Protocols? Mission-critical saves? Safe shut
downs? Lost data? Corrupted drives? Lost time? Company time?"

{ }

Org chart even-stevens, Osgood and Fortman needle each other frequently
and unmercifully, exchanging verbal and emailed barbs like dedicated mutual
nemeses, each assaulting the other's battlements with innuendo at every
opportunity. Osgood reserves sarcasm for the frequent occasions when he gets
the upper hand.

{ }

"I'm aware of that. I'll send a disciplinary memo to myself–immediately after
hell freezes over?"

"Apology accepted. This close to lunch there probably wasn't anything major
in progress, but I'll have my intern check on it and let you know if otherwise.
Then you can blow your section's entire contingency fund recovering our data.
Later!" Osgood punched the button to terminate the connection, snickered,
and turned back to his monitor. "System's coming back up. Hmmm, I see
Branson's whole connection is now gone. Enter!" He smacked the Return key.

Barb peeked in, slow and cautious. "If you didn't know already, the whole
system is rebooting." She waved a sheaf of orange interdepartmental envelopes,
made eye contact with John and held it, unblinking, as she walked the few steps
to Osgood's desk. "Should I hide these until after lunch or do you want them
now? They're marked 'Immediate Attention Required' like most everything
around here."

"I'll take 'em, but don't log them in till two-ish." Osgood grinned, took
the stack from her. He thumbed the corners to check the integrity of the
security tape seals, and arranged the envelopes parallel to the front edge of his
immaculate, simulated walnut credenza. "I already know about the network
glitch. Fart Man didn't warn us. I blistered his ears just now about it. Issue a blue
alert and ask if anyone has a major problem, and if so send a none too courteous

email to Fortman and let him know what was damaged. Sign my name to it and copy Beakman on it. Maybe next time he'll alert us." Osgood twitched. "Door closed, please. John and I need to discuss some security measures before lunch."

With a puzzled look, Barb slipped out and shut the door behind her.

{ }

Alerts appear as small windows on the corner of every screen in every cubicle in one or more workgroups. They have priority, and they stay there until acknowledged with a click of the mousebutton. Blue alerts are informational–Recreation announces Team Kramden volleyball schedule, network admins warn of scheduled downtime, resets, that sort of thing. Yellow and orange alerts are reserved for Security–capital "S." Anyone can issue an alert, but above blue you'd better have a damn good–not just good, mind you–a *damn* good reason for doing so. Plus, it's best if you have clearance from the Power That Regulates Alerts–Fortman.

"She's dying of curiosity," Osgood gloated. "He thumbed through the papers. "Ewww. Red security tape on this one. That's QA."

"Highest level." John chuckled. "They never use anything else. And I don't think she's that curious. The babe's just in heat. Craves my bod."

"Oh, bad. Bad, bad, bad and getting worse." Osgood speed-read the curt contents of QA's envelope. "We urgently have to do something about the future shock, to coin a phrase, that we–I mean the future *schlock* that WE set in motion. Kind of me to share the blame, don't you think?"

"Mere clock ticks now register on the Richter scale for vibes." John shook his head. "I should have known."

"Electronic clocks don't tick. We also have to hope Security hasn't detected or recorded any of the activity associated with my efforts just now, especially the server reboot Fart Man just caused." Osgood grinned, punched the intercom. "Problems, Barb?"

"Minor grousing, nothing significant. Early lunchers took care of it. Everybody tries to get out of here early on Fridays, you know."

"Good. I know this is a weird request, but could you run over and check Brockton's station personally, and make sure there's no one there. G-1853. Just in case."

John raised a finger.

"Oh, sorry, I meant Branson," Osgood said to Barb. "Could be something fishy. Make sure he's not there, by some miracle or Security lapse and that his terminal is not doing anything. Let me know, and alert Security immediately if he's there, or if you see anything suspicious." Osgood turned to John. "Any other ideas?"

"Nope." John stopped smiling. "Besides lunch, that is. Might as well go out with a well fed ulcer."

"Well, I've got one, meaning an idea. Suppose we tell QA–quick, before anybody asks too many more questions–that you previously developed a similar intranet program for an outside consulting client. Moonlighting is frowned on in our contracts here, you know, so you did it before you came to work at Kramden, see? Anyway, we'll say you own the source, in some other language, so all you had to do was convert it and bring it up to date. We can say adding the wide area option was my suggestion, and that you pasted in code that someone else had already worked on–Halroyd? He does that kind of thing in his sleep. Team effort, you know."

"Go team! Excellent story, but not a word of it true."

"Oh, it's worse than a simple lie, it's a cover-up lie of the worst kind, and it's a lie to hide mistakes, which makes it even worse. As lies go, in fact, it's got everything bad going for it." Osgood's eye twitch shook his face. "Cover ups never work, you know. Lunch, eh? What did you have in mind?"

"That spicy barbecue you like too much? Heart attack cheeseburgers? Hibachi? Oh, please not Thai again after the feud you had with them last week."

"'You can't make it too hot for me.' I've learned my lesson. Maybe some day my innards will recover."

"Predictive Analysis isn't a mistake," John said, "but using its output was a serious misjudgement on my part. With all the mad scientist movies I've seen, I should have known better. That's what happens in every one of them. Someone invokes an advanced technology that biped society–whatever planet they're on–isn't ready for, can't understand, and doesn't anticipate the consequences of. The situation varies, but the mistake is always the same. Even Stewie Griffin knows better. Anything but tofu and edamame, even burgers."

"Your choice, since you're buying," Osgood said, stood up, and glanced at his monitor. "Uh-ohhh. New emails from QA just now. Don't they do lunch? No fried chicken, please. We already exceeded our bird quota this month. I'll copy these QA emails to you. They're confidential as all get-out, so you haven't seen them, okay?

{ }

Taco burps, unlike any other burps, bring out the best in computer programmers. For one thing, they express–well, they don't express anything, they just offer the opportunity for a hearty, heart-felt, air quality threatening, environmental impact statement-worthy burp.

{ }

"I can't believe I let you talk me into eating lunch in the company canteen," John said, burped. Loud.

Osgood led the way into his office and closed the door. "We had to do something fast, and that was fast."

"Fast becoming an afternoon of stomach distress." John burped again, excused himself.

"Well, next time La Fiesta, and I'll buy."

"Your generosity overwhelms, but remind me to order something digestible." John slumped into Osgood's upholstered side chair.

Osgood sat at his desk and quickly tapped in his passwords to check his messages, ignoring a row of blue alerts. "Oooo," he said, twitching mightily. "This isn't good. Just while we were gone there's been a string of inquiries–from QA and everybody else down the line." Osgood tapped the envelopes. Now they're even demanding their emails be printed out, initialed and returned. Pfffft. 'Who authorized major development costs before any of it was even requested by management?' 'How did your group access confidential documents where that feature was being discussed?' 'Does somebody over there have access to our private emails?' 'Has company security been breached?' It gets worse."

"Ewww. How worse can it get?" John sighed, picked up the stack of paper memos from Osgood's laserprinter. "That's the consequence I failed to evaluate before unleashing my advanced technology. Just like in the movies. I totally forgot about company politics. I thought they'd be glad to get a jump on our competitors for a change. But no, they're fretting about petty personalities instead of getting the product out to the customers."

"You expected different? As long as you've worked for huge software companies? For Kramden?" Osgood's eye twitch shook his face. "I'm not signing those and sending them back. Shred them when you're done reading. Or take them to the head with you and use them for all their worth. You're correct about company politics taking over. I suspected as much, but I just didn't think they'd latch onto it so fast." He tossed a neatly stapled four-page memo into John's lap. "Get this: 'How can a major project be done in a day, when everything else we do takes months?' See? Safe bet they'll start expecting everything to be finished in a day."

"Ouch. What can we do? What can I do? I don't plan to predictive-analyze everything I do. Or anything else, in fact. Ever." John stifled a burp.

"Agreed. So, we tell them a little fib. No, a big lie, or a little one, a few fibs or a whole pack of damn lies sufficient to cover both of our respective asses. And not a single one of our lies has anything to do with Predictive Analysis, which is the truth, because we can't tell them we can predict the future. We don't mention Star Wars, or Martians landing on the front lawn by the reflecting pool. Lies, lies, and more lies, because they're not ready for the truth, couldn't handle it, and don't deserve it."

"Truth or lies, will they shut up about the tempest in their teapot? Doesn't look good from here." John laid the laserprints on Osgood's gleaming, mostly empty desk. Burp.

"Maybe not." Osgood thought a long moment. "Hmmm, I can probably make it politically not to their advantage to pursue it any further." He leaned over and straightened the stack of paper, aligning it with the edges of the desk. "I have some contacts down there–people who owe me favors, big time. Bet I can reverse the heat–accuse them of wasting company time with politics instead of passing the program on to marketing. They haven't ever cared about the process of getting products created, so I can imply that they're intruding on proprietary processes and invite them to get busy on something more productive. I hope."

"I doubt it'll simply stop there. It'll be like opening a can of Pandora's worms, I'll bet."

"You're a gambling man all of a sudden?" Osgood opened a desk drawer, scooped the stack of papers into it, and snapped it shut.

"Safe bet." John shrugged.

"Probably. Meanwhile, we have this issue of breaching their almighty security. That's a terminally serious topic around here, as you know, and if we try to cover that up we'll be in deep doodoo *when-not-if* we get caught in the lie. But what can we do?"

"Another 'we.' Thanks. But Oz, before 'we' get too much further into this, it's not really we, it's me. I've got no family to speak of and few friends other than you and Stan and the guys who play in *The Safe Sax Sons* on weekends. Why don't I just go bat out a yellow memo and tell QA the bald-faced truth, which they won't believe–leave you out of it altogether. I'll tell them to take this job and shove it, resign in a huff and go get a job across town or across the country, or in Austin or some other suburb of hell, probably for more money and with a lot less stress? No security bots, no Fart Man. No regrets."

"And no Oz," said Osgood. "'We' it started, and 'we' it stays," he said, firm. His eye twitch belied confidence. "From these memos, I'm pretty sure there's no way out for me, either." *Twitch.* "Besides, I get off on the challenge."

"No you don't."

"Okay, I don't." Osgood burped, stuffed his hands in his pockets. "But I can't have you working for someone else. I need you here at Kramden to bat out the complicated little things we–It would take months to train someone to replace you, and–Well, I just like you too much to let you leave."

"From the looks of those memos you might not have a choice," John said, uncharacteristically quiet.

"If we go down, we go as a team, Team Osgood-Farmer, and we go in style."

"Not even Brooks Brothers knows such style," John quipped. "Well, I hate like all hell to suggest this, but 'we' could use Predictive Analysis to find out what QA's going to do before QA can do anything else. It'll be like consulting a gypsy."

"That's just about guaranteed to get us—me—in even worse trouble." Osgood's face twitched. "Unless. Hmmm. Unless we run it outside of Security's ability to track it, somehow." He put a finger to his temple, sighed. "We do have to be extremely careful. Whatever we find out, we're not supposed to know, so we'd act on the basis of that knowledge, and something would happen as a result of that action, and we'd be right back changing the history of the future's past, as you so eloquently put it. Good grief, now you've got me worrying about that future stuff." Osgood eyed his terminal. "Barb's still signed out for lunch."

"Maybe it doesn't matter. Changing the future, I mean," John said. "Maybe you can only change the present, which in turn affects the future and by doing so defines the past. I mean, the program continued to predict your exact actions after you knew of its existence. Maybe it can predict the future in the state it will be if we alter it with itself. In the present."

"If that's not a mind-boggling concept I'd hate to hear one that is." Osgood pushed the stack of memos into the shredder beside his desk. "But we can't run the program on the office networks without getting caught."

"It doesn't need the company's machines. It can run on a single box, as long as it has plenty of resources."

"Number-define plenty?"

"Some-nix Nineteen Dot Two Dot Three, same as we have here, plus a few teras of memory and a gig of disk. Nothing major. Petaflops and gigs of gips are wonderful, but my home system runs it just fine, though slower, of course."

"Of course."

{ }

Gigas are billions; teras are trillions. Petas decillions, meaning thousands of trillions. Just as atoms are discrete chunks of elements like aluminum and argon, (insert-consonant)ips are discrete computer instructions. A Mip is a million discrete computer instructions, and a Gip is a billion of the things, and so forth into astronomical numbers with more zeroes in front of the decimal point than mere humans can easily count.

Although we use computers for many other things besides calculating, their ability to perform simple arithmetic on decimal numbers is often an important measure of their relative power. Flops are discrete mathematical calculations–floating point operations. That's down at the hardware level, before somebody's ingenious software makes any of it make any sense, but the rule is simple: the more the merrier. Lots of flops, good. Not many flops, well, a flop. Lots of ips–mips, bips, whatever–good. Not many ips, wait a long time for anything useful to happen. Like Congress.

Computer math is diverse and complex. Well, math itself is diverse and complex, so it figures. Floating point operations happen with complicated numbers like 3.5, 1.41428571, 28.54, and 8763029314.2. All of these–flops and (consonant)ips–are tallied with *per-second* specifiers to describe computer speed and power. For example, a billion per second, trillions per second, etc. Flops and <whatever>ips are generally indicative of computer hardware *oomph*, meaning raw power. More than a few million of either one is "super." More than a billion is capable of running the better computer games. Trillions of them are the stuff of geek dreams, and petas–well, Hal only wishes. So far.

{ }

John chuckled. "I had some very interesting experiences with Predictive Analysis while developing it. A laugh a minute, sometimes."

"I'll just bet."

"I mean, over the webs during testing." John winked. "The program can quickly profile anyone who's typing in real time, so I signed in as a lurker in some chats and applied Predictive Analysis as a bot to the most active participants."

"Whoa! Sounds interesting. And?"

"After a couple of minutes, it was supplying verbatim predictions of what the people would type next, even predicting what they'd type to their followers on the side, which was even more interesting and sometimes racy. The scroll got over fifty lines ahead in a hurry." John grinned. "Perfect, letter for letter, even the netgeek jargon, the misspellings and abbreviations, and the brats' funny capitalization, of course."

"Of course." Osgood lowered his gaze and raised his eyebrows, questioning.

John held up both palms. "I only lurked, I promise. The people never knew I was there. I was afraid I'd freak them out."

"That's a safe bet, but you missed your big chance to become an urban legend. I'd have freaked them out. Couldn't have resisted. Knowing what they'd stick on their Facething pages before they did it. Priceless."

"On a bigger system with more Gips, the back scroll would get a day or two ahead fast." John smiled.

"So what are you telling me?"

"Two things. If we could secretly pipe the keystrokes from QA's terminals into my program, we could roll time forward, so to speak." John took a breath. "Also Runinhere37 on the IRC channel I visited is a potential child molester as of tomorrow six-ish. I think he's in California, so Pacific Time."

Osgood shook his head. "I'll be sure to keep a lookout. And suppose we warp QA forward in time, what then?"

"We could look at what they're going to type tomorrow or the next day, or even next week. Your root access would let us do that."

"Traceably so, yes." Osgood grumped. "Traceable as all get-out in fact, as you know. Best not make this security breach issue worse than it already is, and very best not to make it so easy for them to catch. I trust you notified the police about the molester."

"I can't, yet. He or perhaps she—you never know—hasn't yet typed the stuff I caught him-or-her typing. That'll be tomorrow when Roy, or whatever his real name is, gets home from school and whips out his pop's laptop."

"Future time. I forgot." Osgood sighed.

"That's why I think we can get away with tapping QA's time-line. So to speak. First of all, there's zero chance they'll believe that we can look forward in time. That's impossible, and they know it—or think they do. In fact, if we told them we could see their future memos they'd have us committed."

"Awww, a commitment ceremony right here among all our friends." Osgood leaned far back in his chair and propped his hands behind his head. "Hmmmmm."

{ chapter 5 }

Chapter 6 : Truth tellers tell tall tales

John thought a minute, too. "The best place to hide something is in plain sight. Gospel according to Ed Poe, anyway. So, why don't we just tell them the truth, which is much easier than making up a lie." He winked, wicked. "No way they'll believe the truth, so we hit them with it. Bald-faced."

"Not bad, interesting." Osgood waved his hand in circles in the air. "Keep going."

"Of course we have to be careful not to tell them the *whole* truth or the *real* truth, or they'll sic the company shrink on us and send us off to the funny farm. Mainly, we can't let them have an inkling that there really is a finished program that can look into the future. The military dweebs would clamp this place down so not even they could get in, and we'd have to surrender source code, executables, the harddrives they're on, everyone's inalienable rights and our soiled underware."

Osgood chuckled. "All to be stashed away in a closely guarded warehouse with the Arc of the Covenant. But go on."

"Short of that, we can vaguely refer to some things they might somewhat understand, and tell them the usual line of "we're working on it, and it isn't out of alpha yet, so we'll send you a memo when it is." John mused. "We'll tell them it's an application of 'artificial intelligence.'"

Osgood interrupted. "Pffft. Isn't all of it?"

"Good point, but we'll enhance it with finger quotes and hush-hush security caveats to the rafters. Projecting what it would be like if we really had such a project." John checked Osgood's eyes for encouragement. "Most everybody–everyone around Kramden at least–has heard of AI, maybe even bitten off some of the hype."

"For good or evil, yes." Osgood warmed to the idea. "I've got it. We'll say there's an experimental, um–, help me out?"

John brightened, continued, "Computer Assisted Inference Engine Development Program?"

"Yes! That we finally decoded from the Area 51 artifacts and we're developing for the DoD's, ummm, highly classified Project LUMK-ATCH for Operation Bandersnorf, and we're testing–no, we had to test it–no, they made us test the prototype–on a real-world application to prove its worthiness for top-secret development funding. Black column, of course." Osgood leaned back in his chair and stared at the ceiling. "It's still early stages," he continued dreamily, as though formulating a report. "Mission critical security levels, the usual crap."

John cleared his throat. "Notice we started this by telling truth, but now we're far out into fiction, and not even a big jump to get there."

"We'll call it K-AIEDT," Osgood spelled, schemed. "That way we can pronounce it, 'See-eight.'"

"Converted to Kramdenese, K8, pronounceable as 'Kate.' Acronyms that can be pronounced are the best, even if they don't have any consonants."

"Exactly. With such a short acronym it's bound to seem extra important. Of course it's so secret that nobody is permitted to even know it exists, much less ask questions about it. Easy to dodge inquiring minds." Osgood leaned forward again. "How'm I doing?"

"That's good so far as fiction goes, probably sell a million copies, but for us right here right now, it's too full of holes. For one thing, Kate would have to have something wrong that makes it unsuitable for future use–secrecy isn't enough. We don't want the DoD clammering for a demo."

"You're right," said Osgood. "Okay, we'll say it crashed, took out some valuable resources, and has to be redone from start. I can stage a few minutes of system downtime and delete a week or two of Security's bots' files to substantiate that." Osgood winked. "Yes, John, I can do that undetected."

"Yikes."

"We'll put out a memo that forbids invoking the program without approval of the DoD-Kramden Liaison Office for Continuing Projects Oversight."

"Which doesn't exist."

"Bingo!" Osgood snapped his fingers. "We'll say it's still buggy–everything always is–and much too dangerous. Requires a pool of anti-matter that it draws power from, and the entire world's supply will only run it for two minutes."

"It wiped out its source files when it ran amok, and some genius we had programming it managed to patch it and get it working but had to go back to his family in Lower Wherovia and got killed in a train crash, and his source code fell into the hands of suspected Canadian techno-spies, but it's double encrypted for security and only he had the passwords."

"Admirably creative, John. For someone who's opposed to falsehood on principle, you're doing a pretty good job of making up a big lie."

"Truth, skillfully told, is indistinguishable from purest fiction." John grinned. "I forgot who said that, but if nobody did I'll claim it for myself."

"And fiction is a Bald Faced Lie by a euphemistic name–like advertising or statistics. I said that, and I meant it. What do we stand to lose anyway? I mean, other than getting caught and getting in worse trouble than we already are? And getting fired? And never again being able to work in software development on this planet?"

John grimaced. "Forearmed, see? We have the real Predictive Analysis. We can know what they're going to do before they do it."

"I already know what they're going to do, and without any Predictive Analysis or statistical analysis or psychoanalysis or anything else: maximum bitching, minimum constructivity. Nineteenth Floor considers them an onerous expense, and I can see why. QA's so predictable I often wonder if they're not just a bot."

"Office gossip has it that way, yes," John said.

"Well, entertaining as your idea is, I'm for doing nothing until we absolutely have to do something. I just wish your software time machine would go backward and stay there, because I really wish we hadn't sent them that program. The comments in your source code refer specifically to memos that no one has written, even yet."

"Ouch. I forgot about those. Do you think they'll read them?"

Osgood took out a white, starched and ironed handkerchief and mopped his brow. He answered John's question with a major eye twitch and a look of extreme nervousness. "They never do, so we can hope and expect that they won't this time, either. When Documentation Development gets the stuff, the dates will still be there–Sourcecode Control, you know. Once it's in Sourcecode's clutches, not even the end of the earth could change it. Documentation isn't likely to bother checking any of it. They never do. They spend days documenting features that were deleted from the programs weeks earlier."

"Hmmm," said John. "Any way we can intercept those emails? Nah, forget it. Bad idea."

"Come in." Osgood shouted at the door.

Barb peeked in, cleared her throat, knocked on the inside of the door. "Mr. Branson is at the entrance having some trouble at the security desk and asking for you, personally. They'd like you to come over there."

John stood up. "Branson? You're kidding. It gets weirder and weirder. I'm out of here. Nice to see you, Barb."

{ }

Osgood's urgent voicemail had John at the office, hair still wet from showering, more than an hour before anyone else would even think of showing up for work. Animating screenblankers on the ubiquitous workstations beamed an eerie gloom into the task-lit space, the only signs of life in the enormous, cubicle-lined, windowless cave that comprised the programmers' section. The lowly coders often worked late into the night to complete their assigned tasks before deadlines, and thus were privileged to show up late. They usually did, if at all possible. Very early mornings were relegated to the housekeeping crew, when the insistent noise of vacuum cleaners wouldn't disturb anyone's thought pattern. Or computer game.

"Brought you something," John said at the employees' entrance, handing over a sack of Krispy Kreme donuts still warm from the fryer. "Jelly ones left, and some plain. I ate all the chocolate. Sorry."

"Wow, thanks, John. You know I love the heck out of some jelly donuts. You're coming in mightily early." Harker, the security guard, waved John through the electronic gate with hardly a glance, even though the metal detectors blinked and beeped like doomsday was nigh. "Must be deadline time again."

"Something like that," John said, winked. "Green-tag this briefcase, will you. I've got to sneak it back out of the building this afternoon with a bunch of company property in it, and I don't want any hassles at the security desk."

"Right. Glad to oblige." Harker affixed a brilliant green "SECURITY 1" tag to the briefcase's handle. He was supposed to open it. Check the contents for contraband–drugs, company property, porno, memory devices, smart phones, recordable computer media, whatever. He was supposed to inventory everything inside it by serial number and individually yellow-tag any employee goods that could be mistaken for company property. He was supposed to hold the contents up to the security camera and tap the toe-operated "go" switch. He was supposed to require written explanation, on Form SFD-4109g rev. 8/2005, of anything that looked even vaguely like computer code and generate log entries on the security section's terminal for all of the above. He was supposed to obtain a biotag–an electronically scanned thumbprint generated by a officious networked contraption–and examine any printed documents for possible Kramden Company proprietary information. That policy–covered in bold type in the Kramden Company Technical Employees Manual, page 2–made printouts of computer source code into Hotel California inmates. Namely, you could bring them in, but they could never leave. Mere humanoids lower than a vice-president or a section manager were never supposed to receive anything higher than Orange level tags. Green tags were *carte blanche*, nigh onto unchallengeable, good for passage through the security portals in either direction, still subject to further challenges but not likely to be checked.

"This tag says it's okay with me if you cart off the whole damn company," Harker said. "But if you do that, please leave the water fountains and the Pepsi machine. I get mighty thirsty standing here, especially when I have to pull a double, like today."

John pretended to scribble on an imaginary notepad. "Leave... Water... Fountain... Got it. Will do. I'll go ahead and leave the Number Twelve Grit toilet tissue in the bathrooms, too, just to be nice." He winked, pocketed the imaginary notebook with a flourish, and grabbed his briefcase. With a thumb-up gesture, he headed off to the programmers' commissary, emporium of antique pastries, coal-oil coffee, powdered espresso, and half-stale sandwich fare dispensed from a row of vending machines along the inside wall. Shades of Horn and Hardardt.

{ }

Obviously shaken, Osgood slupped coffee from his personal ceramic mug. Company logo on the side. "There you are," Osgood said, checking his watch. "Good morning."

"Some might call it good, maybe, but I don't know who," John quipped. "Morning to you too, and early morning at that. Much earlier than I like to admit to ever being awake." John plunked his heavy briefcase onto the table and noisily dragged a gray plastic institutional chair out from under the table.

"Green tag, I'm impressed. Harker never trusts anybody with a briefcase after that exotic hardware heist last year, and he never green tags anything. Not after those customized CPU cards vaporized in March, along with nobody knows what else."

"Must be my honest face," John said. Besides, I bribed him with fresh hot donuts. Lifetime supply, eighteen-wheeler load. Chocolate frosted. I used your Visa card number to order them, hope you don't mind."

"Cheap at half the price," Osgood said. His eye twitched. "Green tags don't come lightly. But, did you get his cardiologist's approval for all those donuts?"

"No, his wife's. She's got a thing for me, and with him out of the way..."

"Ha! I haven't met Harker's wife, but I know your taste. But we won't go into that. Especially not within these company walls, and with company sexual harassment policies keeping company lawyers up nights. Anyway, here's why I panicked." Osgood's eye twitched, fast. "Beakman's onto something, or thinks he is, and Fart Man isn't far behind, still trying to figure out those Branson incidents." He pushed a coffee-stained memo across the table. "It gets even worse. I'm sure you'll agree stuff like this gives me reason to panic, and I'm sure you'll agree that panic is the correct term for this... this...."

"State of mind? Yep. Panic's the right word. I already have an idea what it says," John reached for the page. "Should I sit down first?"

"'Fraid so. Our worst fears weren't worse enough." Osgood watched John's green-eyed glance bounce across the terse memo.

"Ouch."

"Can I cut you a slice of fresh company coffee while you recover? Extra cream and sugar, right?"

"Extra cream, extra, extra sugar. Thanks."

"Extra, extra sugar. Got it." Osgood pulled a large foam cup from the rack.

"Ouch," John repeated, louder, tapping the memo, as Osgood returned to the table, balancing the brimful cup.

"What do you make of it?"

John slupped coffee. "Let me think a minute. Hmmm. I should have bought more donuts." He slupped noisily again. "Another minute... Okay, a lot more thinking would be even better. Can you call me late next century?"

"No time for procrastination. We've got to do something quick. I mean, today, right now, before anyone comes in to work. Don't you agree? We've just got to do something, and now."

John stared into the coffee's bubbly surface. "Got to?"

"Either that or start clearing out our desks, mine particularly."

John gulped the coffee. "I see that. It's way serious. Definitely needed to buy more donuts."

"And our other options are?" Osgood's twitch shook his whole face. "You brought it, didn't you?" He looked at John's briefcase.

"Predictive Analysis? Stupidly, yes, I brought it. It's installed on the laptop ready to run, freshly optimized on my home system. I've got some real problems with using it, though—reservations. Second thoughts, you know, and third thoughts, and thirtieth and so on. This is not a good idea."

"We have no other choice."

"Oh, there are plenty of other choices, but you—that is, we—don't like any of them." John drained the last of the coffee. "I should have bought more donuts."

"Confidentially, John, this is a very shaky time for me. Financially, I mean. Right now, I can't withstand even a small interruption in salary, and I can't see how this latest development wouldn't interrupt my salary—our salaries, need I emphasize?—unless we head it off. I'm up to my ears in debt. A month, six weeks, and I should be able to plan for it. I'll spare you the whole gory detail." Osgood's eye twitch shook him again.

"Debt. Been there, done that. Couldn't afford the T-shirt. Nah, don't bother with the details. Too depressing. But, I would've figured you for certificates of deposit, automatic savings. Beefy IRA, vested profit sharing, that sort of thing." John looked at Osgood's hands, which gripped his coffee mug.

"All that, yes, of course, but I'm out on a limb with some, er, investments that haven't matured. Some opportunities opened to me just recently that might not have been available in the future. So, well, I'm invested to the hilt, and cash flow is a serious need right now."

"Gambling, in other words? Gambling *debts*, in even other, other words?" John smiled empathy.

"Stocks, bonds, futures, hedges, it's all gambling of one kind or another anyway. You're betting the economy won't lag, betting the stock goes up, the market for the product doesn't die off, the CEOs don't get caught with their hands in the till, the auditors are on the ball, and maybe the FTC was awake when the corporate reports came through. You're betting the technology doesn't go obsolete before the product even gets packaged, the patent office smiles on you and some competitor doesn't object to every tit and jottle of the application. You bet the FCC or the FDA, or the whatever else acronym doesn't hold up their approvals for some bureaucratic quibble. Really, it's all a big gamble."

"You mean like waking up in the morning?"

"That too. But some of the stuff I'm in right now is pretty risky. Most of it, really, but if only one of them pays off I'll never again have to deal with another corporate memo, or write another security report, or kiss any more Nineteenth Floor ass."

"Dream on."

"It's a dream, but it's something." Osgood twitched violently. "I just need a month. A couple of weeks, even."

"Say, this isn't some Nigerian money laundering scheme? You didn't fall for that old Spanish prisoner crap?"

Osgood bristled. "I'm not stupid, just invested to the hilt."

"You guys need anything?" Harker passed by the commissary's vending machine wall on his security rounds.

"Not right now, thanks," John called. "We might need some help carting out the larger computers later on, though."

Harker laughed as he swiped his credit card sized activator into the networked barcode reader beside the commissary entrance, then punched in his four-digit code. "Four-one-seven-two... Shit... Four-one-Seven-TWO," he muttered. "Forget it, John, I'll sneak into the executive gym and do some curls and stuff tomorrow before my shift. Right now, I'm not lifting anything heavier than this card. I'll just filch a forklift from shipping for you." The card reader emitted a friendly triple beep, audible throughout the room.

{ chapter 6 }

Chapter 7 : Unwitting co-conspirators

O sgood snorted as Harker checked the electronic lock on the hallway door. "A forklift, he says. Some security we have around here."

"Actually, from our point of view, excellent security," John reminded. "He also said, 'Four One Seven Two.'" John jotted tiny numbers, backwards, with his ballpoint onto the palm of his hand, adding two to each digit. He patted the briefcase. "Need I point out the difficulty of getting stuff in or out of the building if there were any real security?"

"Granted."

"Besides, the electronic systems around here are the real risk. With the right passwords you could take more from this company than you could ever get out the employee entrance, even with a fleet of forklifts."

"Too true." Osgood's twitch took over his face for a long moment.

John showed off the numbers in his palm. "Just in case we need it, and I hope we don't, but my gut tells me we will. My old laptop's in the briefcase under some papers. It's never been connected to the company networks, never logged into the building, and not traceable by any means that I know of. It's expendable, too, so if I–we–can't get it back out, it can just get 'lost' or tossed in the compactor, and no big deal. Everything on it is encrypted past Neptune, so by the time anybody figures it out we'll be tottering around in an old folks home somewhere."

"What a thought. You know I'll insist on a designer walker."

John stood up. "Let's decide what we're going to do if anything and do it. Please, before I change my mind and lose my nerve. Or both."

"Good idea." Osgood took the briefcase. "I'm getting really nervous."

"I can tell. And me, too. Oz, do the security cameras in the hallways record sound or just video?"

"Ouch. Good point. I'm glad you asked. Inside this building they're video only. We can talk freely in the halls. Just in case, though, try not to face any of the cameras when you speak–lip readers could wreck us. Security doesn't have that ability that I know of, but the DoD might. Umm, John, do you have a family–other than the one guy I met?"

John led the way through the corridors toward Osgood's office. "Just my brother, that you saw with me at SIGGRAPH in Chicago. No wives, no children–that I know of. No significant other, contrary to office gossip."

"So if it comes down to taking the heat for what we're doing, or for what we have done, or for what we're going to do–?" Osgood covered his mouth with his hand, pretending to stifle a couple of coughs so the cameras couldn't record his mouth movements.

John smiled, turned toward Osgood, conveniently away from the cameras' gaze. "If you need to, lay the whole thing on me, and I'll deny everything and resign in a huff. It's my program that's causing the problem, and it was my foolish use of it that created all the trouble. No point in both of us going down with the proverbial ship."

"Thanks. I'm not going to do that–never even considered it. I just wanted to know." The coughing ruse again.

"I've been saving up for a while, looking to get a couple of new synthesizers and some MIDI toys. Nice ones. With that fund, I can easily withstand a hiatus in salary. Adjust my lifestyle, maybe take a few music gigs. No sweat at all. In fact, I could use a break."

"Wish I could say the same, and I'm going to make that so. Soon, I hope." Osgood's eye twitched. "Anyway, I'm in this for the whole ride, all the way, all or none. I'm a gambler, and this qualifies as one hell of a gamble."

"I hope this particular gamble pays off in something besides trouble."

"For a change." Osgood feigned a cough. "This is ridiculous. Remind me to delete the damn surveillance video files. That server can just have a root problem so we won't have to carry on this charade. Anyway, it's going to look suspicious if we cough every time we get close to a camera."

{ }

"Fart Man's onto something for sure, but he doesn't know what." Seated at Osgood's desk, John typed commands into his laptop computer as Osgood, twitching constantly, looked over his shoulder.

"P9 that's right. Then tilde, lowercase r, dot, three zeroes... that's it. The next one is the same, but exact reverse order."

"I way far don't like the tone of tomorrow's memos from Security. With all the intrusive bots they have, what we're doing here seems extremely dangerous. You're certain they can't detect this?"

"It's off in the next galaxy from what they know about," Osgood assured.

"Untraceable? That's a rarity in this system, as you know."

"You forget that I wrote all the security modules, back when I was in your section before I got kicked upstairs, so to speak. I requisitioned these accounts for a new hire who was going to telecommute from Vancouver. She got a better offer, or pregnant or whatever, and never started work. Anyway, I, uh, left the budget where it was. Semicolon, not colon. That's right. Then three zeroes. Her accounts have stayed active, and no one checks them. I set up a background task to renew date flags on some dummy files in her allotted space to keep auto-delete from flagging them. She's totally beyond Security's scrutiny because she never showed up for work and didn't go through their biotag system. They don't even know she exists. Which she doesn't."

John backspaced to replace a character.

"Anyway, we can cruise around in the system on her and some other ghost accounts without causing any curious logins. Beyond that, you really don't want to know any more."

"Deniable plausibility. Thanks. I might need that."

"The hardware was the limiting factor, but your unknown laptop fixes that. No way I could do this from my terminal. As it is, the logs won't know this session ever existed after it's disconnected from the network, and the system will think no new allocations have occurred." Osgood twitched, smoothed an imaginary wrinkle from his coat sleeve. "A brilliant plan, if I have to say so myself, and I wrote a wicked bot to carry some of it out. And that's all I'm telling about it."

"We're in. Whoaaaa, group-wide access. I'm impressed."

"You're actually in much further up than that. The power in that particular login reaches far beyond the walls—a substantial enhancement I managed to add yesterday. Er, with some optimizing that I did on the bots. I knew we'd need it to reach QA's files from an unsuspect account."

John typed administrative commands warily. "Good thinking. Devious, dangerous thinking, but good for our devious, dangerous purposes."

"Okay, here are QA's new memo files... their emails... time warped to three days from now. I'll grep around in here for anything interesting."

"You can print to my laserprinter with impunity. It's local to this connection, not on the network." Osgood smoothed his hair nervously. "Wait! That email... cat it. Print it. Tomorrow's filedate... confidential..." Osgood stamped his foot. "Those shits!"

"Yup. Ewww, looks like we're in for a wild ride." John typed the print command, but backspaced over it. "No shredder," he explained to Osgood's quizzical look.

"Right. Good thinking. Pipe to flex. No, don't. Best not to leave a trail of any kind. I'll just memorize it."

"Let's see what they do day after tomorrow. Were you able to capture anything from their terminals? We need something we can use to initialize the Predictive Analysis program."

"Here. It's named 'slash-cap' on this optical. Rot 13." Osgood produced a plastic-encased CD-Rom disc from his inside coat pocket.

"Rot 13?"

"Just habit. The slash prevents the automatic backup system from getting it, you know."

"Cute. I'll suck it in from the cd, which I'll pretend I don't even see since it's writable media, to keep it off the system. We'll flush the disc in the men's room on our way out of here." John typed into the terminal.

"Better to flush it from the women's room across from QA."

"Mega-devious," John said, laughed. "I'm proud of you."

"Running Predictive Analysis version 0.9.6," the screen display read. Half a second later another line blinked on screen: "Loading resources... 1G... 2G... 3G... Accessing resource file... Error."

"Oops, redirect from Rot 13." John typed furiously for a few seconds. "That did it."

"Erasing file. Formatting rewritable CD, DoD level 9 secure," the screen read. A maroon window appeared.

"DoD Level Ninety Million isn't secure enough. We still flush the damn disc." Osgood twitched.

"Agreed. Okay, the program's analyzing... accessing profile... storing revised profile—here's where traceability could screw us... and... ready to predict." John poised his fingers over the mousebuttons. "What do we want to know?"

"Okay, Mister Gypsy, look into your compiled crystal ball and find out what they're going to do, say, Thursday. We can probably infer what they do today from what we find out they're going to do tomorrow and the next day." Osgood's eye twitched as John brought up succeeding lines of memos that Quality Assurance wouldn't type for days.

"Looks pretty tame." John clicked rapidly. "Still tame... man, they lead boring lives over there... Tame, tame... boring. Oooo, racy letter to boyfriend... regarding another boyfriend... interesting... but no time for that now. Uh-oh. Now they're getting nasty. This is... tomorrow, four o'clock. Bunch of clock watchers. They've done virtually nothing since noon and now they're burning us just before they go home for the day. Redirect to laserprint. Think we should print this one out while we're here."

"Shredder?" Osgood reminded.

"We'll flush it."

"Okay, but use small type so it won't take too long to get rid of. Not cool to get spotted coming out of the ladies' room. Ohhh, remind me to check if there are cameras in that area."

John typed at the terminal, fast. "We'll take another quick look at Friday, too. I must admit I still think it's creepy to look forward in time like this."

"Creepy isn't the word for it, but it'll do for now... looks like they're in bigtime nasty mode Thursday. Ewww, all day Thursday—not much else going on in their section other than this security breach crap. Soap opera... soap opera... All this is a repeat performance from tomorrow's rantings, so probably nobody's listening to their bitching."

"Safe bet. Who ever does listen to QA's bitching?"

Osgood propped a hand on the desk beside John's mouse hand to lean in for a closer look at the memos piling up on the screen. "Check Monday, then? Won't hurt since we're already here."

"Safe bet they don't darken the office doors on weekends, but the program takes that into consideration. More racy boyfriend stuff."

"If you want to look even further on, feel free. I'm absolutely certain that what we're doing on this terminal is completely undetectable."

"Ummm, I'm not so sure," John said. "Look at this... an email to security... network access... password breach... they've changed their passwords twice a day and somebody's still getting through to read their email, which of course is what we're doing right now without their stupid passwords."

"We are, indeed, but in the past. Do they know we have a time machine? Would they believe it if we told them?"

John rolled the mouse. "Nope. Looks like Security doesn't know about this session, fortunately. They insist on believing somebody's sniffed their precious passwords. Look at this one... They're not sure it's us, but they suspect our section, because of my intranet program. The boyfriend stuff is undoubtedly what makes them so sensitive—see this email marked confidential?"

"I've covered my tracks. They'll never find out about this account. It's far above what they can access. We have to remember not to mention the stupid boyfriend thing, even in passing. Err, who's the boyfriend in question? Anyone we know?"

"Ooops. No way. One of them is Zach. You remember Mister Marketing? Slick dude. Too slick. I can't believe he's dating Miranda in QA. She's hot on the outside, but a total iceberg where it counts."

"Doesn't put out, eh?"

"Ha! She puts out plenty, but far *too* plenty, and it's always her terms all the way, and her terms are... well, you don't want to know, I promise."

"Great gal. Glad I don't know her. Uhhh–?"

"Oh, sorry. I was distracted for a sec. Predictably, their emails are obsessed with the Miranda and Zach saga. Big scene in the parking lot tomorrow morning... Zach with a bruise, and everyone wondering if she gave it to him..."

Osgood cleared his throat.

"Well, that'll be all over the grapevine in fifty different versions. I'll just skip to some more of their memos. Hmmm. Looks like they're making a big deal about some guy named Bivens. He's not in on the boyfriend thing, but Miranda's all upset about him. Ohhh, I see, now. Looks like Hal Bivens, whoever that might be, is getting blamed for what we're actually doing. Heyyy, he's in our section. I've never heard of him, and he's a very seedy character, it appears. Foreigner. Do we have anybody by that name?"

"Not a real person, no, but a Hal Bivens has an account on the networks. He's fiction, an employee name I created to do some, uh, testing in the security system when I need to." Osgood smoothed his hair.

"Again I don't want to know any more?"

"Again you don't, you really don't." Osgood smoothed his sleeve again, his eye twitch violent.

"So here they're talking about memos they sent and got curt answers from Beakman. Nothing unusual. Isn't he the cooperative one? Obviously doesn't have a clue, but thinks he does." John rolled the mouse. "Beakman's son is in on the boyfriend thing. He has a son? Nasty kissoff message from Beakman Junior to... there's only half of it here. We're straining the program's ability to predict. It needed more training time."

"Half is already too much if it doesn't relate to our own predicament."

"True. Anyway, here we are at the end of next week, and... whoa! Look at this! Bivens is getting fired. Wait! Bivens has already been fired, and they're wondering who got him."

"That's it, then." Osgood looked at his monitor. "Blue alert on my regular terminal. Someone's here–probably Fart Man. We have to sign off this connection soon." Osgood went to the door and locked it.

"I'm hurrying. Redirect ROT 13 to flex. Nevermind the paper. Too much flushing to do already." John yanked the laptop's power cord and packed it into the briefcase. "Meet you in the commissary shortly. I'll detour by QA and flush the disk."

"I'd better go flush it," Osgood said, rummaging in his desk. "The cameras are being monitored at the Security desk by now, and they don't need to see you in that area. I can drop off these intra-office envelopes and look official doing it, so they won't suspect."

"Good plan."

"I'll destroy the surveillance video archive around noon. No one ever checks them unless there's a problem, so we'll be okay. They won't even know they're gone for a while, most likely."

{ }

"No donuts today?" Osgood handed John a cup of hot coffee. "Extra cream, extra-extra sugar."

"Thanks. I need it. Too early for donuts, and too much of a hurry to stop anyway. What gives now?"

Osgood sat down. "The usual. It's Beakman this time. He's been poking around in places he doesn't have permissions to poke. Don't ask me how I know. I just do. He's bugging me for passwords to get into the video servers. He somehow found out the archives was hosed, and he's determined to find out who did it."

"Ewww."

"I stonewalled him, of course, but he's getting more suspicious by the minute. I say we lay this whole thing on Bivens and let him get fired for security violations, maybe have him try to take some company source code out in his lunch pail or something. And then the whole thing dies down, finally. We hope."

"Fess up, who the hell is Bivens?"

"He's fiction, a Canadian contract hire, like I said. Kernel level developer. Credentials up the ying, McGill *magna cum laude* and all that. But I made him up. Got him an ID badge as a temporary contractor to work on benchmark improvements... the badge is in my drawer there... he's cleared for telecommute from Ottawa when he's not here–log-in account to inside the firewall, *et cetera*. He's in your section for all anybody knows. I just reassigned him there until we get a new hire to replace Branson. Except he doesn't exist and never did."

"Excellent, I think."

"Bivens is just what we need. I'll assign him some optimization projects that require him to root around in the system, so to speak, give him high level access and control over the surveillance camera servers. With permissions like that, nobody would dare get too quizzical about him. Except Beakman. Then Bivens can get fired for tinkering with QA's emails and bringing down the video servers to cover his tracks."

"Promise me you won't ever take up writing detective novels."

"Huh?"

"That story has so many holes in it, even the holes have holes." John laughed. "Sorry. Don't mean to deflate your fantasy."

"What holes? I can assign Bivens a permanent cubicle, like he's been here for months. Set a bot to log him in at the front gate at varying times every morning for the last few months–yes, I can do that too–and log him back out at four or five o'clock. The logs are purged quarterly, so we'd only need to generate logs since first of quarter. Then it wouldn't be hard to set him up to take the heat for this whole tea party. One of QA's boyfriend emails 'accidentally' gets sent from his terminal to someplace it shouldn't go, and the video servers go down again–super easy to do. QA finally finds out who hacked their passwords and gets somebody to barbecue, so they're happy. We get them off our backs, and we're happy. Bivens doesn't exist so he's happy, too. Then after we have him unceremoniously escorted out of the building, the so-called security breaches come to a sudden stop. Therefore logic clearly dictates that Bivens, like the butler in those detective novels, did it. The end."

"How can we have Bivens escorted from the building? He doesn't exist."

"Simple. You can get his Contractor's ID badge out past security. Past Harker, that is. You've already got the green tag to do that. Then anybody could come in with it, because nobody's ever seen Bivens, since he doesn't exist. We'll get somebody to play him for a day and be escorted out. Too bad Branson is known around here. He'd be a perfect."

"The whole idea is too dangerous. A strange face appearing all of a sudden that nobody knows–they'd call in the cops, not just Security's goons. Besides, that means we'd have to involve someone else, and trust them to pull off the whole skit flawlessly. That never works, even in the movies. Somebody would ask too many questions and get too few answers. Whoever we get would run into his former girlfriend, or boyfriend as the case may be, working in the commissary or something and that would be the end of our charade. Besides, people would want to know why nobody's ever seen him before. And how is it he commits a firing offense the first time anybody ever lays eyes on him? And who could we trust to play Bivens and keep a secret that big? Definitely nobody in this company."

"Good points, all. But maybe Bivens doesn't have to actually be escorted out for it to work. Aim your prediction program at Security's main terminal, and see if there's anything we shouldn't know about that we can read." Osgood's eye twitched as he handed over a optical disk. "Here, I went to the trouble of setting a bot on them yesterday to gather this email session. You can use it to train the program."

"We were only going to spy on QA. And you did what?"

"Yeah, I know. It was underhanded, and yes I can do that without leaving a trail. So, don't look at security's terminals, then."

John typed some commands into the Predictive Analysis window. "This is a dumb thing to do, I just know it."

"He says as he does it anyway." Osgood walked over to the door and checked it. Locked.

"The accuracy goes mushy with only a results file and such a minuscule training session, you know."

"I know. Hey, Fart Man is in way early, working frantically in his office—the blue network alert hasn't gone away yet. So capture his session and store his 'profile.' He can't see anything that happens on this terminal."

"Wicked," said John. "Just wicked."

{ }

In the familiar grayness of his cubicle, beyond the reach of a rusty dawn that intruded through distant office windows, John carefully packed his laptop computer back into the padded womb of his briefcase. "Oz, are you sure we should leave this thing in the building? What if Beakman gets inspired and pokes around... again. We're no longer above suspicion. Stashing such incriminating evidence in my cube makes me way nervous. Not to mention lack of sleep from getting here before daybreak so often."

Osgood patted John's shoulder gently. "There, there. It'll be all right. Everything's going to be fine, really it is, John. It's just that we've had to hack the system more times than we expected, to keep the big mean ol' company from firing us."

"Every two days for over a week. Way more than we figured, for sure. And for what? You know how many job offers I've received since this infernal program ruined my sleeping habits? There's a cozy stack of them on the kitchen table at my apartment, waiting to be answered."

"That explains the sudden increase in the department's laserprinter costs. Sending out some résumés, were you?"

"Didn't you?"

{ chapter 7 }

Chapter 8 : Job search materials

"**E**xactly, Oz. Beautiful shirt, by the way. Hawaiian print, I like those. Is that silk? Way nice. Don't tell me you haven't put out any feelers yourself? That's so not like you–the shirt I mean. What happened to your upwardly mobile gray flannel look? Is pink the new gray? Pineapples the new pinstripe?"

"Okay, I sent some résumés out too, I confess. But let's just try to hang on another week at least, somehow. Thanks for noticing. I bought this Saturday in San Francisco with Stan. It's quite comfortable. No use for boring gray any more, since I'm not looking forward to being with Kramden much longer."

"Super workmanship. Snazzy design. Goes well with those black shorts. Gave up climbing the corporate ladder, eh? A touch of vertigo? Oz, I'm really looking forward to getting out of this place, and only trying not to leave in the middle of a security purge. It would look bad." John coiled the laptop's AC power cord neatly around his palm. "Besides, even if we manage to extricate ourselves from this tempest I don't want to slave away in this teapot forever. It's time to move on, anyway. To something better, maybe. No offense."

"I gave up climbing this corporate ladder right after we raided Fart Man's terminal that last time. The writing wasn't on the wall, it was in his private memo to Nineteenth Floor. It doesn't seem worth it any more. No big loss. HP?"

"May be."

"Not the dreaded Microsoft? Surely not you of all people."

"Worse than death." John smiled broadly. "How do you know about those? Did they call you for a reference? The corpladder where I'm seriously considering, like the proverbial elevator here, doesn't go all the way to the top."

"Okay, so don't tell me."

"Still making up my mind, but it's a very small company, way much smaller than this one. It's super laid back, too. They develop software and hardware technologies for game boxes, smart phones and gambling devices, and they license the finished products to other people to market. Zero layers of bureaucracy. Zero marketing dweebs like Zach and his pals to deal with. And no big Security blitzes, and no DoD. Unless warfare is reduced to computer gaming, they have nothing the DoD wants. The owner comes to work just like the rest of her people and sits in the same office. Real offices, too, not just cubicles. There's so much less hassle. No security cameras peeking out of the rafters or any need for any. Same salary and benefits, but lots more freedom."

"Freedom is what you get when you don't work for anybody anymore. Well, maybe till your parents kick you out of the house for freeloading?"

"It happens." John smirked.

"Ouch." Osgood eye-twitched and winked at the same time.

"I'd be writing interfaces to their proprietary 3-D graphics engines. They use a pseudo code similar to the one I built into Predictive Analysis so they can easily port their games to whatever hardware they're writing for. They can bring their whole line of games to a new device very simply. It's brilliant. But much as I like that one–the offer, the job, and the hot babe I interviewed with–I might not take it. But I haven't made up my mind."

"Can't blame you if you take that one. It sounds really nice. John, if you need it, I can pre-date a resignation and accept it so you don't have to hang on through a notice. Might be wise in view of our tenuous circumstances here."

"I was hoping you'd offer, and I had a feeling you could engineer just such a scenario. But right now I'm still thinking. I have, um, other offers to consider."

"Just let me know. I'm planning to do the same thing for myself if we don't get in any more trouble. And speaking of which, what are we going to do when-not-if Security catches on to our latest shenanigans? You saw that memo just now. It's only a matter of time before both of their neurons connect."

John sighed. "You mean, what do we do other than get hired someplace where the security staff is a big friendly dog? I guess the only thing we haven't already tried is to hack into the system and destroy their records."

"Aha!" Osgood tapped his forehead with his palm. "Why didn't I think of this Wednesday when the laptop was connected?"

"Whoaaa, this escalates the situation far beyond deniable plausibility. I'm not destroying anybody's data, especially not my own."

"Self defense. Destroy, or be destroyed. It's like a big role playing game, only the roles are us and the evil alien invaders are Fart Man and Beakman."

John opened the briefcase again and uncoiled the power cable. "And QA, with Zach the wuss looking on and gloating. If he gets the babe, that is."

"Now?" Osgood glanced at the clock. "You're not about to delete–? They haven't caught us, yet."

"Preemptive strike. In modern warfare, self defense or otherwise, if you acknowledge any rules you've already lost. We'll have to do it eventually anyway, so why not now. You saw Beakman's memo and Fart Man's reply. 'The source of the problem has not been directly traceable so far, and that leads me to believe it originates with the programmers who originally created Security's crawlers and other systems.' That's you, you know. And me, and Branson who's already gone. I say we turn the whole server system to mush now while we still can, before we have to do something even more risky. Even nastier." John poised a hand over the mouse.

"General Brown is not going to like this."

"Herr Brown, Mister DoD Head of Security, never likes anything, especially not me."

"Nor me either, way not me either. It's a sure bet we're going to be blamed for this, too." Osgood wiped his fingertips on his shorts.

"At this point, we'd be blamed for stuff we didn't even do, so we might as well do it. I'm tempted to run over to my cube and save my work off to opticals, but if I do I'll be the only one who doesn't suffer from the disaster, and that might be a disaster all its own. I know what I did and how I did it, so I'll just suffer with everyone else, and redo it. What's wrong with this machine? All of a sudden it doesn't respond."

"Come on, it was running just fine." Osgood examined the laptop's power connection. "Is it getting power? Wiggle the cord."

"Nothing. I'll try to reboot it."

"Disconnect the network cable before you boot it. We don't want it to announce itself just yet."

"Wait a minute! You remember that last sequence of commands? From a few minutes ago connected to the network? It makes sense now!"

"What does? Ummm, another blue alert. We'd better not sign onto the network with that machine from here again. I can do the global file delete from my terminal with a background task. I've been able to optimize it considerably lately, so no one will know."

"Those PC prompts, and those commands–I understand, now. Oz, you bastard! You installed Predictive Analysis on the company network, didn't you? And it's still running. Why didn't I recognize those commands earlier? Now we really are in a world of trouble."

"A world of more trouble."

"It's all clear now. We couldn't count on getting my laptop out of the building past security, since we couldn't depend on Harker's being on duty every time and didn't dare ask. So we were leaving the briefcase in my cube, and later locked it in your office cabinet. And you... you..."

"I hooked it up in my office without your able assistance."

"Ha! And?"

"And I ran your Predictive Analysis program and used it to help me optimize a few of my bots, including the one I used to capture Fart Man's email sessions over the network without getting caught. *Mea culpa.*"

"And?"

"And... *Mea* some more *culpa*... well, I also found out some things that I shouldn't have known and shouldn't have found out, and I know the future, which is not good."

"Things such as, Mister *Tea Culpa* To The Max?"

"WF Tech, Illinois. Some Chicago burb. Are you mad at me?"

"That's the offer I'm seriously considering, yes. You've been peeking and poking around behind my back. At me! But why?"

"You're the program's default subject, and I couldn't help looking. But that's all, just that much. I figured you were leaving, anyway. I switched to other users immediately and didn't look at yours any more. I promise. John, I had to do something quick. I got called in to Beakman's office, and just had to know what was going to happen. Turns out it had nothing to do with us, fortunately. But while I was at it, I tried to figure out that mysterious memo that Fart Man sent to Nineteenth Floor day before yesterday. You remember the urgency it had about it, but Harker looked in and we didn't get to read the whole thing. Anyway, from Beakman's phone call I thought we might be doomed right then, and I had to do something quick. There wasn't time or opportunity to get you in on it, so I took matters into my own sweaty palms."

"My program knew I was leaving. That's how you found out."

"I suspected. Doesn't take a predicter program to figure that out. Working conditions here aren't the greatest, you know."

"Agreed. Okay, what else did you find out that you shouldn't have found out that maybe I'd rather you not know, or maybe rather not know you found out?"

"I found out what your former neighboring cube mate was doing all day when he wasn't working on the code I assigned him to do. Branson?"

"I don't want to know, and really, I don't care, either. Oh wait, I remember. He had some online lady friend he was 'seeing,' sort of... eastern European somewhere. You mean her?"

"No, the stocks. Please don't be too mad at me, although I totally can't blame you if you are."

"Stocks? I never would've figured Branson for a gambler."

"Not a gambler, an investor. Like me. He's shrewd, too. Very shrewd."

"Gambler big time, shrewd or not. Now I get it. You found out... okay, how much did you lose? Or make?"

"Plenty. Much, much plenty, and plenty much more after that, and redoubled that plenty two or three more times," Osgood bragged.

"Positive plenty I assume, from that mule-eating-briars grin on your face and the unannounced trip to San Francisco and the cool new duds. So, when are you moving to your new ranch in Maui?"

"Branson's *culpa*, too. He somehow redirected your program off the network the day you showed it to me. He only ran it once, but he was able to clean up, and I do mean clean up, in bonds. The reboot we did stopped his fun, or he could move half the women in all of Eastern Europe to a high-rise here in town. He couldn't retrieve your source code, because Security stopped him at the front entrance. Remember? If not for that we'd be contending with a serious contender for Villain of the Year. I'm sure of it."

"So that's why he kept reappearing at the gate asking for you. He was making the calls, and you provided the predictions–for how long, Oz? Truth!"

"I only ran the program itself yesterday. Branson was working on that single set of data files that he created the day you showed me the program. He couldn't get to the software from outside the building–which he wasn't cleared for anyway–so he tried to defeat the firewalls using a back door he'd built in for himself. But Security caught him and wouldn't even allow him physically back in the building. He's the investor. I've just duplicated his buys to the best of my financial abilities. And as of now my financial abilities are much advanced. I only used the program to second-guess Beakman and optimize some bot code. I should have alerted you, I admit, or at least warned you."

John frowned.

"I humbly apologize for being a shit, if that's any help."

"Don't tell me any more. I don't want to know. So that's why you shouldered the blame for the whole episode so readily."

"Partly. Never underestimate the power of a DoD security investigation to ruin a perfectly good investment plan. Or a gambling binge."

"And that's why you converted from ultimate skeptic to total believer so fast."

"Yup. Branson was too smart. I should have known that when I hired him for intranets. He was brilliant at what he did, but too smart for his own good."

"I didn't get to know him." John folded his hands in his lap. "But then, I thought I knew you pretty well, and I wouldn't have figured you for this, this. This whatever it is."

"Branson didn't like to mingle with mere humans. Had his eye on the stars, as they say. Wrote back doors and system hacks into everything he did, but when it came down to it, his arrogance got him caught. Thought he was smarter than he really was. He hacked your account and snagged your program while you and I were using it in your cubicle–he overheard our conversation, looked through his logs and diverted streams to his account. That put a sudden drain on the group's resources that he thought Security wouldn't notice. Wrong. He only had time to have the program generate a bunch of future closings for some stocks and a few key commodities that he's been watching for years. Then he made his big mistake–trying to get the massive log files out of the building. His quickie hacks to bypass the firewalls brought down Security's bots, they thought it was company information since he obviously generated it on company time, and that was that."

"So, if Branson didn't get the program out of the building, or the source code, then how–?"

"When he got locked out, he could only take advantage of the information he could remember from the predicted logs, but that was enough to generate substantial profits. Fast."

"So he called you in. I remember Barb saying he was at the gate asking for you. A couple of times, in fact. I should have suspected you right then–taking a risk like that, talking to a known security risk. Not like you at all."

"Right." Osgood held up his hand to keep John from talking. "I promise I did not grant him access to anything, or give him any files, or access to your program, which wasn't running on the system until a couple days ago. And I immediately expunged those prediction logs from the system. He'd heavily encrypted them, anyway."

"So how did you profit? And Branson?"

"We made a deal. Branson and me. He gave me a list of the back doors and hacks that he'd installed in the intranets system, and I patched them, and documented the fixes for Security. In return, I gave him the predicted numbers for some items that he wanted. I retrieved his logs from the automatic backups, applied the encryption keys he gave me, and extracted a list of numbers that I relayed to him."

"So you used the program's results, but not the program itself."

"Yes. I needed the information about the vulnerabilities in the intranets system, and traded the predictions for it. Not even all of them, actually, just a few that he said would be most profitable."

"And they were indeed profitable."

"Immediately." Osgood grinned.

"And Branson?"

"I kept refusing to give him the program or its source, and he cashed out. He said it was smart to take profits and leave, so I did that too. He insisted we take our profits out slowly, so as not to poison the pond or leave a trail. Don't want to be accused of insider trading. That's a bigger crime than fluorescent lighting and gets you more jail time than axe-murdering your butler. I've already paid off some big debts, thanks to your program–and Branson. But there's still plenty more profit to take if I can liquidate it quietly. In another week I'll be fine. No Maui ranch, but plenty fine. That's why I really, really, really don't want to get fired just now. Are you mad at me?"

"I figured you were getting offers from better companies, and couldn't understand why you'd hang on here with this security stuff stewing. Gambling winnings, stock profits, whatever. I should've known. I'm not mad. I'm furious!"

{ chapter 8 }

Chapter 9 : Future speak

Osgood smoothed his growing bald spot with his hand. "I'd offer you a substantial sum as consolation, but I already know you'll refuse."

"You already know? Oh, this is not good. Way not good. Way mad, way bad, way not good."

"It's way not-good-er than that, even."

"How so?" John slipped the laptop into the briefcase and slammed it closed. "It's dead, so there's no bother about it being in the building any more. You can't be trusted with it. I'll take it home with me today if Harker's running the desk. Still got a green tag. If not I'll toss it in the trash compactor."

{ }

Trash cannot merely be taken out at Kramden Software. For one thing, people might put security-sensitive material in the trash–accidentally or otherwise– and retrieve it after Sanitation removes it from the building. Paper, tons of it per week, gets shredded into tiny bits that are randomly jumbled into huge containers–so all the bits of a single document are unlikely to end up in a single dumpster. The dumpsters are combined into trucks that haul them to different incinerators according to a varying schedule–so no one ever knows the fate of any given load of trash–just like network television. Company gossips claim the resulting ashes are then propelled into deep space, but that's only gossip. Electronic components, mostly from the hardware development division, go through a chopper before being hauled away for recycling. Glass, metals and plastics also get chopped into tiny bits before being recycled. Biologicals– the remainders from the commissary's culinary endeavors that won't fit the Goats–industrial-strength garbage disposers–go along with everything else to the company's solid waste station where Security officiates operation of the trash compactor from hell. It reduces a week of garbage to a small blob nearly dense enough to have its own gravity. Closed, guarded trucks haul the blobs to a landfill at an undisclosed location, where they're immediately covered with tons of soil and guarded twenty-four-seven.

{ }

"John, your program is running on the system, and I can't stop it. My doing, not Branson's. It's running through Bivens's account—remember Bivens? We got him fired for security violations to take some heat off of us. I used his network accounts when I unencrypted Branson's log files. Risky, but it worked. Anyway, I installed it in his account from your laptop and set it running in a protected space so it wouldn't affect the rest of the system. That's what's so not-good. I can't stop it, and it's sitting in an account that not even I can delete. Those commands? They're from when I invoked it on Beakman's memos. And Fart Man's. I've already looked ahead extensively. But I haven't been able to stop the program, although it is parked, fortunately."

"So, not only is my program operating in the future, you are too, and it's running on the company's resources with no way to stop it."

"Might say."

"Might say, hell! Any idea what the stock close will be tomorrow? The weather? The next earthquake?"

"Not funny, John. Way not funny. Your program is running in Bivens's account, and I can't delete all of its background tasks. I tried this morning to make it close down, and it wouldn't, and I have good reason to doubt we'll be able to close it today, either. Is it me, or do I sound like a fortuneteller?"

"Three mouseclicks."

"Tried that. Look, I can certainly understand your being steamed at me. I let you down and betrayed your trust, and I apologize."

"Control-Q? 'Steamed' is an understatement."

"Tried that too. It wouldn't break with Control-C either, but that did stop it from restoring itself to the console. It's still there, John. It protected itself. Trust me on this."

"Ummm, Oz, while you were peeking and poking around in my laptop, did you look at my source code by any chance?"

"Yes, but just enough to make it compile within Bivens's allocations."

"And?" John took a large book from a shelf in his cubicle.

"And I... well, I had to modify a couple places to make it run in a protected window and not trigger any of security's bots, and without making itself known to the oversight utilities. I used those network options you left unchecked."

"Those were disabled because they behaved erratically, as you no doubt observed." John scooped an armload of technical books off the shelf and piled them on the desk.

"John, what are you doing?"

"Packing. I suggest you do the same." Frown.

Osgood twitched. "No need to pack, yet. The predicter program predicts we'll get in, and it's right, of course. Besides, you said yourself you can't leave in the middle of a security hassle. It would look bad. It says we get in, so we get in, laptop or not."

"Of course. Who are we to tinker with the future's past? But how? There's no time to go to my apartment for the backup drive, and no time to replace it, which is no easy task in this old laptop. And that's assuming Harker's working the gate and it's possible to get the other drive into the building. It's not feasible without getting caught. I can tell from your smirk you have a pat answer ready."

"Easy, John, your blood pressure's off the Richter scale. Since I've unintentionally left it installed on the system, we can run it from the network itself. Log in from my terminal as... as Bivens. We do our damage as Bivens, and then exterminate the program, which I hope you can figure out a way to do, and then I'll create pre-dated resignation notices, and we can leave in good graces."

"Did you forget you had Bivens fired?" John opened his personal effects drawer and scooped its sparse contents into the box.

"Doesn't matter. I found out a lot of useful stuff while I was running Predictive Analysis. I erased Bivens and edited him out of all the logs. He doesn't exist and as far as anyone knows never did."

"I know you've managed to improve the security privilege on your accounts considerably, but how about the backups?"

"I can obliterate them, easy. I have access to virtually everything, now. Well, not virtually anymore, actually everything. It's expanded a lot lately, as you so perceptively observed. That optimization pass worked wonders."

"Actually everything. Talk about power."

"Thanks be to Branson. John, what you don't know will be of much more value to you than what I won't tell you."

"Well spoken. To your office, then. Unfurl the pirate flag. Captain Oz the Hacker sails the software seas. Won't even Harker get suspicious, though? I mean, when his terminal display vanishes before his eyes? We're the only ones in the building besides him. Even he will figure out that it's us."

"If he suspects anything, it has little to do with computers. Harker undoubtedly thinks you and I are getting it on in the executive washroom before work. Screw Harker."

"He's not my type."

"Good point. We could stage a power outage. That would help cover the damage I'm about to do."

"Oz?"

"Yes?"

"All the computers are battery backed. A power outage wouldn't do anything but turn the emergency lighting on. Sexy for a tryst in the hallway but useless otherwise. Besides, the real damage is already done—a dangerous program running on the company's network with no way to exterminate it. We can't leave it, we just can't."

"That's it, John, you're a genius."

"Thanks, but... Oh, wait, I see what you mean. We'll create a runaway task that brings the whole system down. When everything comes up again, my program can't restart itself, so it's gone, and Security's files are long gone, along with any records of what we do to bring it down."

"As well as the backups."

"Of course. But, don't you already know this from reading the future with my program?"

"Some of it." Osgood looked sheepish. "Forgiven?"

"Some day," said John. "Maybe. Actually, I'd be a lot more steamed if I hadn't been up to no good all this time, too." He stepped into Osgood's spacious, prim office, snapped the lights on, and seated himself at the terminal. They left the door open.

{ }

By Kramden Company protocol, a closed door means a high-level meeting is taking place. Everywhere except HR itself, it also means there have to be three or more people present, because two people isn't enough for a high enough level meeting to warrant closed doors. The open doors policy is meticulously spelled out in the company conduct manual and profusely referred to in the company's sexual harassment policy statements. Section 22.

{ }

Osgood sat down. "I knew we'd be doing what we're doing, yes. It all makes sense, now. And I know we're going to–"

"Oz, look, just... just don't tell me any more of the future. I'd rather be surprised. Heyyy! How's it going?"

"Damn. Oh, good morning, Mister Harker! How are you?" Osgood's eye twitched violently.

"'Mister' Harker? You're mighty formal this morning. And decked out in shorts. Vacation time, Mister Osgood?"

"Just getting with the spirit of things, Harker. Uh, how's your wife?"

"Fine, I suppose."

"You suppose?" John looked up, bemused.

"Well, I didn't ask her this morning. She's a whole lot easier to get along with when she's sleeping, so I let her sleep."

"Got it."

"John, we don't want..." Osgood whispered, pretending to point to the screen.

John shot him an assuring glance. "Okay, see you, Harker. Oz and I have to finish hacking into the company coffers before the place opens. We'll text your pager when we're ready to sneak the large bags of cash out the side door."

Harker chuckled. "Good idea. Wouldn't want just anybody handling all that loot." He strolled out and swiped his card through the security reader just outside the door. Beep-beep-beep.

"Whew!" Osgood's eye twitched rapidly. "I was afraid he'd invite himself in for a chat. Can't have him looking over our shoulders at a time like this."

"Relax. Harker's dependably aloof," John said. "Besides, it's one or three yards over here, much more exertion than he'd expend just to be sociable."

"And what's with his wife?"

"Bipolar."

Osgood twitched. "Ohhh. I can relate."

{ chapter 9 }

Chapter 10 : What y'mean, 'we'?

"Myparanoia's probably unfounded, but I'm being careful," Osgood said. "He says as we attack the very gizzard of the computer network."

"So to speak. Did you get in yet?"

"Yes. We're in. Note the present person plural?"

"We. Got it. I apologize for letting your program get out of hand, and I apologize for running it in the first place, and I apologize for making mounds of cash with Branson's information, and for not telling you all about my dealings with Branson, and for not cutting you in on the profit potential, and–for all of it, really. I had a greed attack and then, well, I have no excuse."

"Nope. No excuse. No scruples, either. I haven't yet decided whether to forgive you, but there's no time to debate that right now. First, the program is indeed running, but parked. Other than hogging system resources, which is likely to set Security poking around, it won't cause any trouble. We still have to delete it. After what I sense is our imminent departure, I don't want the DoD getting hold of and weaponizing my software. And second, judging from the content of these files I'm deleting, we are indeed in great danger of not having lunch on corporate soil, if you get my drift."

"I noticed," said Osgood. "But I also know that tomorrow... well, never mind."

John looked up, still typing commands. "If it weren't for the fact that Predictive Analysis is still on the machines, I'd would already be out of here, security hassle or not, fired or not. But there's no way I'm going to leave the program on this system, for reasons I don't have to explain." John punched the backspace key with a vengeance. "We, and I do mean 'we,' will deal with the errant predictive program after we zap Security's files–in the hope that WE can stay employed long enough for at least me, if not both of us, to exit gracefully."

"I just hope we can, on all counts. I wouldn't blame you if you just escaped. John, if you just want to depart now, I'll figure out a way to cover for you so it won't look like you did anything. You can cite some relative's illness. I'll set a bot to create some memos with dates of a month ago. Whether you forgive me or not."

"Oz, I just can't leave any part of the program on the company systems. And I can't explain exactly why I can't right now, but you'll understand soon. If you've run the program far enough into the future you already know anyhow, but I still won't tell you." John typed furiously on the keyboard, tapping the backspace only a couple of times.

Osgood watched the door, silent.

"All right! Zapped," John exulted. "Totally screwed—and that's them, not us, for a change. They'll give us no more problems temporarily. We've set them back at least two days."

"Good. So far."

"So far, yes. But there are crayon markings on the wall. We're doomed, not for this shenanigan as much as for stuff we didn't do that we're being blamed for in memos that they're going to write this afternoon. I suggest we plan our departure as soon as possible after the Bivens accounts are history." John smacked the return key. "Security's system going down in..." John looked at an imaginary watch... "Tee Minus Fifty-leven Milliseconds. Done. Now the automatic backup and restore processes will only get day-old stuff. They're way screwed. Man, this is power."

"Careful the power doesn't corrupt you," Osgood teased.

The whole facility plunged into darkness, and the building's feeble emergency lights came on, throwing their reddish beams at ceilings and floors, some of them giving out an insistent beeping, an indication of poorly maintained batteries. Throughout the offices, the battery backup power supplies set up a frantic beeping of their own as screens blinked off and displayed only "System Reset" in tiny letters in the middle of black screens.

"It already has. Now, let's remove the errant program. Do you remember exactly what source modules you altered? Here's the file list. Screen only, sorry. Can't risk a printout."

Osgood's eye twitched as he moved in close to read the list. "I have almost total recall for things technical. I edited that one, and changed the load-management parameters in those three. Nothing else."

"Those three? What three?"

"Those."

"You're sure? Oz, those are not part of my original source. They were on the laptop? Those are not my modules."

"They're not?"

"Nope. Trust me on this. I have almost total recall for things source code."

"Oh shit, not again," Osgood muttered as Harker peeked in.

"You guys still at it? Aren't you ready with those money bags yet?" Harker stuck his head in at the door. "Good thing the power interruption didn't get you, eh?"

Osgood straightened up and stood behind John at the desk. "Battery backed power supplies to the rescue." His eye twitched.

The lights came back on, but the frantic beeping continued, for the most part.

"I don't know if we're on the emergency generators or if the power's come back on," Harker said. "Those battery backups have a short life. I'll go check the security console if you need to know."

"Won't matter," Osgood said. "We'll be able to finish what we're doing before the batteries go out."

"Darn moneysack program keeps crashing," John said, cheerful, not turning around. Out of sight under the desk he pressed his hand against Osgood's knee, an urgent gesture that screamed "keep still."

"Whole damn security system went down when the power blinked off, and now it's on the fritz. Gotta wait for it to reboot. Ya want something from the commissary? Coffee or anything?"

"Thanks," John said. "But we'll be heading down there in a sec, as soon as we can get this last program to compile." He typed some gibberish into an empty window for effect.

"Doubt you'll get anything for a couple minutes," Harker said. "Once the security system goes down the whole network waits for a reboot and self-check before it allows any activity."

"Oh!" Osgood slapped himself on the cheek. "I forgot about that, and I'm the one who wrote it."

John jumped, took his hands away from the keyboard.

"Oops," Osgood whispered.

"Well, you guys come on down for some coffee. The system takes a while to reset, you know." Harker ambled away whistling an atonal non-tune.

"Youch! I hope Harker's as stupid as I figure him to be. I really blew it, bad." Osgood mopped his forehead with his shirttail.

"If he suspects anything at all, he's bound to get curious and catch on," John said. "He could make trouble for us, accidentally even, well meaning lunk that he is. I don't suppose your vast foreknowledge of the future is of any benefit to us on this score, Mister Total Recall of Things Technical?"

"Not that I know of, but if there were anything I'd recall it, wouldn't I?" Osgood smoothed a non-existent wrinkle out of his shirt.

"I hope so. We can't do anything till the system comes back up, so we probably ought to get out of here to keep down further suspicion. I'm sure it would be in our best interest to show up in the commissary and be sociable for one or three minutes. Just wish we had some donuts. I'll redirect to a background task and set a ten-minute fuse." John typed the commands carefully. "This is even better, actually. We'll be with Harker and won't be sitting at any terminal when the main damage is done. Quick, make up something we can cover our presence with if Harker gets inquisitive. We have to be sure he notes the time while we're there, too. Get us out of this one and I might forgive you for getting us into it."

"Working on it, even as you speak."

{ }

"You fellas done all your damage for one morning?" It was Harker. "Here, have some coffee on me."

"Thanks." said John reached for the coffeepot. "The system's still too sluggish to do anything. How'd you manage to get the coffee maker up and running before the commissary staff comes in?"

"Helps to know people in high places–like the cleanup lady. We sit and rap sometimes in the wee hours, and she watches out for me. Leaves the key to the coffee supplies cabinet under the tea urn."

"Under the tea urn, I'll remember that."

"Don't bother me none. Help your self."

"Extra cream, extra, extra sugar," said Osgood, pouring John's mug only half full to allow for the anticipated additions. "Mister Harker, you see anything funny around here this morning?" Osgood winked surreptitiously at John.

"Funny? Other than you calling me 'Mister'? Nope. Not since the system went down. Now that's real funny 'cause it's still early so nobody's here yet. It'll be back up in a few more minutes, though. You can depend on that."

"I mean, why would the whole security system go down?"

"Beats me. Only this section went down, not the other floors, as far as I can tell. Gremlins. Haints. Poltergeists. Gotchas, I reckon. More gotchas in a computer network than there are in an iron clad contract."

"Iron clad contract?" Osgood said, twitched, winked at John again. "Well, it looks funny to me, too. Real funny."

"Uh, is there something wrong that I don't know about?" Harker shifted his weight to his other foot.

"Well, John and I, we were just poking through the system for a memory leak that's been causing our programs to fail. Have to catch those when the system's idle, like early in the morning when nobody's here. And all of a sudden, it's like we're not alone on the system. There's a bunch of other tasks running that we didn't initiate. You know about tasks, Harker?"

"I try not to know much about computers, but I know. They're the–"

"Right. Well, there are tasks running, a whole lot of them, and we can't do what we're here to do, because the tasks are allocating memory, and next thing you know the whole system fails. It's funny, don't you think?"

"I'll say." Harker caught John's gaze. "Extra, extra sugar. There's more in the cabinet. It's still unlocked."

"You're sure we're the only people here?"

"Yep."

"There's no one at security's terminals?"

"Nope. They don't come in this early. Just me." Harker stirred his coffee.

"Then is there any chance that someone could have hacked into the system from outside?"

"Oh! Well why didn't you say so? No. It's not possible. Can't be done."

"Not possible?" John blew cooling breath across the surface of his coffee, which didn't need cooling. "You sound awesomely sure."

"I'm certain. 'Cause until I enable it at six-thirty, all outside access is blocked. It's turned off automatically at four in the morning when the cleaning crew comes in. They don't have access to the software to re-enable it. Only I do. That is, any of the security terminals do, if you know my password. It's that way on purpose, 'cause the cleaning crew, well, they're an outside contractor, you know. The phones are partly disabled during that time, too. Outgoing calls only, except the security terminal, and they route through the old switchboard. It's all part of the security system."

"Correct," Osgood said, twitched, sipped. "Very observant of you, Harker. But that's exactly how I designed the system several years ago. However, today, that is this morning, that's not how it appears to be working. Currently, I mean. Just now. Right now." Osgood's eye twitched rapidly. "Maybe there's something wrong with the switch. It's only software, after all. Does anybody ever verify that it's working?"

"Not that I know of. Can it be disabled? Look, this technical stuff is way over my head. I'll run a self-check on the terminals when they come back up. Let's talk about football."

"I don't know anything about football," John said. "On purpose. Unless you mean soccer, which I'm sure you don't."

"What about them Dawwwgs," Osgood said, unenthusiastic.

"Okay, what about them?" John tore open sugar packets for his coffee. "I'm a cat person, myself."

"I'm bullshitting you," Osgood said. "That's the sum total of what I know about football."

Harker slapped the table. "Awwwww, that's enough! When you know about them dawgs, you know all you need to know about football. Mister Osgood, you are my kinda fella."

"Thanks, Harker, but that doesn't solve the problem. What about our Mister Network Hacker, if there is one? Just call me Oz. No need for formality. Not any more."

"Hacking from outside somehow?"

"I'm afraid so."

"Hacking by Who?"

"Whom," Osgood corrected.

"Whom? Do we have anybody working here by that name?" John snickered. "No, I think it's Branson. Used to work in my group? Remember we had a problem with him trying to hack into the system from outside the building a little while ago. You were at the security desk."

Harker thought hard. "That's right. I do remember Branson. Tall fella. He's still working here?"

"Thanks to a couple hours worth of security memos I had to file, no," Osgood said. "I'm sure it's his login that caused the problem just now. Don't ask me why, but I definitely think it was him or someone impersonating him trying to get into the system that caused it to reset."

Harker took out his pencil and jotted a couple of notes on his logsheet. "Branson. I'll put a note for Far–I mean–Fortman in my log."

"Yeah, let Fart Man know. Add Bivens, too," Osgood said. "He's in cahoots with Branson, I'm sure."

"Bivens," Harker repeated, spelled. "Don't believe I know him."

"He was a contractor. Telecommute from Toronto. Almost never here in person, and he's gone too."

{ chapter a }

Chapter 11 : The corpulent songstress warbles

As the sunset's golden early glow bathed Kramden Software Corporation Employee Lot C, Zone 2, Reserved for Intranets Programming Section, John stacked his worn, green-tagged briefcase and three boxes of computer books into the back seat of his blue convertible. He grinned at Osgood, who was approaching his Saab one parking space away.

"You get a good parking spot when you're the first one here," John said.

"Especially if you get here before daybreak and don't leave for lunch. That is, unless you rate a reserved space, like that Whom guy," Osgood said.

"'Whom was here.' That was your handwriting on the stall wall, wasn't it?"

"Couldn't be Harker's. It wasn't signed with an X." Osgood fished in his pockets for his keys. "I was nice and used water soluble ink."

"A last act of defiance, I'm proud of you," John said. "But don't underestimate Harker. Still water, way deep and all."

"I was just letting off some pressure. This has been one hell of a day, and a hell of a long day, and a hellishly mega-stressful day to cap a bunch of mega-stressful days, weeks on end. I'm actually truly glad it's over, finally, even if we are out on our asses."

"I'd be glad if it really were over." John's cocked hip indicated his doubts.

"It's over. The last vibrations of the large lady's High C have echoed off the corporate rafters, and school is now out. Forever." Osgood flicked imaginary rubble off his wrist.

"Yeah, but the school is a smoldering ruin, and we're the arsonists. And here we are stacking matches into our cars right in front of the place. Do you think they'll try to sue us? Wonder what the statute of limitations is? How long do we have to hide out? Think they'll send the cops after us? Or the DoD?" John stopped packing his car to wait for Osgood's answer.

"No way, Mister Paranoia. At Kramden, the *statue* of limitations is that amorphous sculpture on the front lawn next to the fountain. The company's so busy suing their competitors to death and defending Nineteenth Floor's guilty butts from sexual harassment claims, there's no bandwidth left in the legal department to sue mere peons like us. Besides, we left security so mixed up–thanks to your brilliance with Harker's passcode–they'll be in a stew for years trying to figure out how non-existent people swiped security stations in two different places at the same time. They don't dare raise too much of a stink, or the DoD will demand an investigation, and that would cost the company major money and stall progress on all their projects. Besides, what can they prove? We erased all their memos, as well as almost the whole backup storage. They won't ever know who to blame. "

"Whom." John pointed at Osgood, who crumpled with laughter. "They can prove Harker's an idiot. You don't think they'll fire him, too? I'd really hate that–his wife and all."

"Harker's safe. I managed to change the passcode for his card so next time he comes in he'll look like an innocent babe, even though he'll look pretty stupid for forgetting his password. I'd just managed to make sure Harker was in the clear when Fart Man shut my terminal down. He's in for a big surprise tomorrow around noon. I left a bot running is his own account that's going to make it look like he did what we got accused of. And now that we're gone, it'll look like he's the culprit, not us. Besides, we planted the Branson information with Harker. He'll get a medal for that, and probably a promotion eventually."

"Too bad you couldn't have done the same for yourself. Or me."

"I tried, really I did. Two more minutes and we'd've been in the clear." Osgood stacked neatly packed boxes of books and personal belongings into his car's sparse trunk space. "I knew what I had to do to protect us. Before we managed to exterminate it from the system Predictive Analysis predicted I'd perform those exact keystrokes. But when I typed the command, the terminal was already dead and we were on our unceremonious way down the gangplank, so to speak. The prediction failed."

"Ha! It did not fail. First off, it correctly predicted what we'd have to do to exterminate it. Nice, don't you think? Predict its own demise? Then it correctly predicted what you'd try to type to clear us. You typed the stuff on a non-functional terminal, but you typed it just the same. Predicting keystrokes on a dead keyboard? Wow. I'm impressed and I wrote it." John patted himself on the back.

Osgood came around to John's car, leaned close, and lowered his voice. "John, this could be a security violation for me to talk about, but I'm kind of into security violations lately. Do you know where I'm going from here? I mean, my next job?"

"I know, and I don't know." John smiled, making eye contact and lowering his voice.

"Oh? You know?" Osgood stuffed his hands into the pockets of his shorts. "What do you know?"

"It would be a security violation for me to say, of course." John smiled, holding eye contact.

"Of course. Then you do know!"

"I know, and I don't know, but I know what I don't know. See? Beyond that, I'm not permitted to say, and I know enough about all of it to know that you're not permitted to ask, much less know." John looked around to make sure no one was within hearing distance.

"And if you know, but you don't know on purpose, then it must be that what you know is higher level than what I know. Especially since I wasn't supposed to know that you knew." Osgood smiled knowingly.

"You catch on quick."

Osgood smoothed his hair, which didn't need smoothing. "And if you also know that I'm not permitted to ask any further, then you know what I'd ask about if I were permitted to, yes?"

"Yes." John smiled, lowered his voice some more.

"So, when do you start?" Osgood whispered, beamed, and winked.

"Classified info, but I'm permitted to discuss that with certain co-workers on a need-to-know basis. I've started already."

"I start on the third."

"I know."

"You know? I didn't know you knew."

"Of course not. But I've known longer than you have. I take the blame for getting you hired, if you must know. But you don't know that. Promise me you don't know that."

"I promise I don't know a thing. None of it." Osgood thought for a second. "Mister Supervisor." He grinned.

"'Chief Systems Analyst, Computer Assisted Intelligence Section, Statistical Data Projection and Analysis Team.' But you can just call me 'John.' I'm not one for formality." John looked Osgood up and down. "Don't forget the dress code. Ties are not allowed. That Polo will do nicely. Get some more of them in different colors, but lose the socks. Got any Birks? See you in D.C. on the third." John looked around again, checking for people in the deserted lot. He opened the door to his car. "Don't be on time. I certainly won't. We wouldn't want to give the agency the wrong idea on the first day. Ten-ish?"

"John?"

"We rule, Oz. We don't bow and scrape. Not to corporate ladderdom, not to puffed up executives, not to suits and ties, not to anybody. We rule."

"We?"

"Your modifications to my source code created a program that has them scared. Really scared, and not just them but me, too. You know that."

"I know, but how did they know that?"

John winked. "I told them."

"Do I know that?"

"You can know that."

"Thank you. Now that I know that, why did you tell them. And when?"

"You probably shouldn't know that, but I'll tell you anyway, and after I do, you don't know it. Okay?"

"Deal." Osgood looked around the parking lot.

"Remember those three modules of Predictive Analysis you modified that I didn't write? The ones on the network that got everything out of hand? The ones for which we destroyed the whole network just now, to expel the program from the system. The ones that, in a sense, just got us fired?"

"Those? Sure. You really panicked about those modules."

"Those modules came from some of my early experiments. I contacted the place you do not know about when I first showed you the program. I proved its capabilities to them about the same time we were hacking Kramden's system to find out what QA was going to try to do to us."

"Ah. I remember. But how did those modules get onto your laptop?"

"They didn't. I never put them there. You altered the program, remember? Then your modifications, which you intended to make you vastly rich, caused the program to predict itself into the next state I compiled itself in—which contained those modules."

"Okay, I follow that logic. With difficulty, but I follow it."

"Those modules give the program the ability to do really ominous things far into the future. It not only projects its own predictions, but actually implements them on remote systems, just as it almost did this morning before I brought Security's systems down. If your modified code in those modules hadn't had that bug that let me stop the processes, we'd be way deep in shit, in addition to being out on our asses."

"Bug, what bug?"

"You don't know about that. Remember, you don't know any of this. You not only don't know there was a bug, you don't know what there wasn't a bug in, or even that there was something that could have had a bug. You particularly don't know what the code did that the bug wasn't in. Got it?"

"Got it. But I really don't know any of that, John. You didn't tell me. Wait! Don't tell me—as if you were going to. If I don't know, I won't talk in my sleep and blab to Stan accidentally, and then Stan tells someone at his firm, or his shrink, and, and—well, never mind." A breeze stirred the air. Osgood smoothed his hair and looked over at the orange horizon. "So, what are we going to do at the agency whose name we dare not speak? Finish debugging the bug that isn't there in the module that isn't there, and implement the capability that doesn't exist? None of which I know anything about?"

John grinned. "Oz, you've been hanging around Harker too much. Have your brain cells stopped working? Were you studying law?"

"Hunh?"

"That's his thing. Harker. Or didn't you know? He dropped for a while when his wife was diagnosed, but he's planning to go back to law school in the fall. Oz, what we're going to do at the unknown agency is absolutely nothing. We're not going to write any lines of code or debug any code or push any pencils or fill out any weekly progress reports or–" John frowned "–or make any investments, risky or otherwise."

"Oh, that. In the rush of getting ejected from this place and turning over the passwords and such, I guess I forgot to tell you."

"Oh-oh, what?"

Osgood grinned. "I managed to retrieve almost all of my profits before my terminal deleted itself–before Security deleted it. Offshore accounts in islander banks, safe as their respective dictators permit them to be till a couple of months go by and I can safely retrieve the funds."

"You what?"

"I moved my funds to known safe accounts that I can draw down slowly from home."

"Funds."

{ chapter b }

Chapter 12 : Capital gains

"**A**ctually, you're talking to a brand new millionaire."

"And I thought you were living on the edge. Then, why did you take that job?"

"The new job's a cover. I definitely need the convenience of being able to say everything I know is classified information, in case anyone comes snooping. I need a visible means of support, too, in case any investigative bodies check me out. You do too, in fact, but you've got that covered already. Just in case Harker's supervisors ever put two and three together."

"Deniable plausibility again."

"Exactly."

"I'm onto that, the plausibility thing." John cleared his throat. "And the cash thing, too. I definitely need a cover line, and 'sorry that's classified info' makes a great one."

"You? Profits? I'm shocked."

"Good guitars are expensive. And synthesizers. And saxophones." John smiled, fingering a fast rock riff on an air guitar with his ignition key as a pick.

"John, on what I've got stashed, you could hire the San Francisco Symphony and put them up at the Cupertino Hilton while you await your muse."

"I did okay, too, Oz. Not bragging. Not telling, really, but I'm so not poor. The agency was shall-we-say generous. I'll see your orchestra and raise you a small Pacific island with lots of macaws and a strong tribal tradition."

"You sold them the source code?"

"No way. I wouldn't trust even myself with that code, much less a government intelligence agency. Any government."

"So, if I'm permitted to ask, what did you sell them?"

John smiled, indulgent, wicked. "Nothing. I sold them nothing, and you're not permitted to ask any more than I'm permitted to answer you. True answer, though: nothing. Exactly what you and I are going to do in D.C.. You remember the scene at the end of that big dumb movie? The Ark of the Covenant in a crate being filed along with a xillion other things in some Area 42 warehouse?"

"Area 51?"

"Give or take. That's what we are. The Ark. We're being filed away because nobody's willing or able to deal with the power of what's in the box. My box. Predictive Analysis, version 1.0."

"Pandora revisited."

"Exactly. So, we chill. Us and Predictive, like the Ark, filed away in a window-walled office in suburban D.C., instead of a dismal warehouse, but it's the same thing, really. I insisted on tons of glass. Or maybe we bake in the sun at some beach resort in Hawaii, or crawl the blues dives in Memphis—that's on the agenda, too. Parked like the Ark. You don't mind moving to D.C. for a while? I've never been. Thought I'd check out the museums and the music scene if they have one. For a while."

"D.C. is a hell hole. I've been there with Stan on some architecture things several times. Great museums, though. Extremely high crime, permanently snarled traffic. I don't know about the music scene."

"Okay, we'll hang around till the museums get tired of us and then move the office to... to...?"

"The Big Island?"

"For a while. Lots of great architecture, I'm told. Stan will love it there."

"So will I."

"Oz, you know how I feel about weapons systems. I'm adamant on this. We are not writing any code, ever. They're never to get any source code, executables, nothing, ever. Not a line, not one single curly brace, nor a semicolon, a slash or a star ever leaves my possession again. The agency is basically paying us not to develop anything. That way the program won't exist and I won't sell it to anyone else. But if some other country does start working on a similar system, then we have to tell them how to do it. Not do it, just tell them how."

"Great deal. Do I know that?"

"No."

"For a valued employee, I know very little."

"The less you know, the better off we both are. And the planet."

"Thanks, John. I appreciate your vote of confidence. I'd offer you some of my millions, but I sense you've bested me at profit taking."

"Profit is an understatement." John strummed his imaginary guitar.

"Let's get out of here before they find out the extent of the damage we did to their networks. I don't know about you, but I'm not answering my phone at home ever again. Or the door. Let the voice mail and the caller ID handle the calls. Uh, drop over for a drink, Mister Supervisor?"

John raised an imaginary glass. "To the future!"

THE END

www.ingramcontent.com/pod-product-compliance
Lightning Source LLC
Chambersburg PA
CDIIW050739230626
47052CB00003BA/532

* 9 7 8 1 8 7 9 2 1 1 0 3 2 *